"You _____
David said roughly

"No," Rachel denied, but it was impossible to argue with him. "She told me everything about you. She wouldn't lie. I...I don't understand—"

"Yes, you do. You understand this."

And then his mouth slashed down hungrily on hers. For a moment she fought the sensual intrusion, but then found herself welcoming it.

Suddenly a shrill cry from across the room startled Rachel and she pushed free. "What was that?" she whispered.

He laughed softly. "That was Isis, my pet hawk. I think she was telling us she doesn't like what we were doing."

"She's a smart bird," Rachel said in a voice that amazed her with its steadiness. "Neither did I."

As she hurried outside, Rachel wondered if her lie had sounded more convincing to him than it had to her.

SANDRA MARTON says she's always believed in romance. She wrote her first love story when she was nine and fell madly in love at sixteen with the man who is her husband. Today they live on Long Island, midway between the glitter of Manhattan and the quiet beaches of the Atlantic. Sandra is delighted to be writing the kinds of stories she loves and even happier to find that her readers enjoy them, too.

Books by Sandra Marton

HARLEQUIN PRESENTS

Don't miss any of our special offers. Write to us at the following address for information on our newest releases.

Harlequin Reader Service
901 Fuhrmann Blvd., P.O. Box 1397, Buffalo, NY 14240
Canadian address: P.O. Box 603,
Fort Erie, Ont. L2A 5X3

SANDRA MARTON

heart of the hawk

Harlequin Books

TORONTO • NEW YORK • LONDON
AMSTERDAM • PARIS • SYDNEY • HAMBURG
STOCKHOLM • ATHENS • TOKYO • MILAN

For my father,
who taught me to love the Catskills

Harlequin Presents first edition November 1988
ISBN 0-373-11121-5

Original hardcover edition published in 1988
by Mills & Boon Limited

PROLOGUE

AN UNNATURAL silence lay on the wind-ruffled ridge. Seconds before, the air of the meadow below had been thick with bird calls; now, there was only the droning buzz of insects. A black stallion, reins dragging from his bridle, grazed quietly among a profusion of wild-flowers. A quick smile softened the lips of the tall, broad-shouldered man standing nearby.

'You've frightened all the birds away, Isis,' he said softly, raising his right arm to shoulder height. 'They know we're here.' His left hand rose and his fingers touched the pale grey breast of the hawk perched on his leather-gloved fist. The hawk tossed her hooded head, her taloned feet shifting impatiently. 'Patience,' he whispered, 'patience. I promised you a flight today, didn't I?' He bent his head towards the bird and his teeth flashed whitely as he bit at the laces that closed the elaborate hood. 'There,' he said finally, pocketing the hood. 'The sky is yours, Isis.' His arm rose rapidly. With a flap of her powerful wings, the hawk rose into the air, circling steadily upward, her leather jesses trailing after her, their tiny bells the only sound to break the stillness.

The man lifted his gloved hand to his eyes, shielding them from the sun, watching until the hawk was only a dark speck against the cloudless sky. Gradually, the sounds of life returned to the hillside and he smiled again, the smile changing to a frown as the cough of an engine intruded. He watched, expressionless, as a jeep pulled

7

up the hill and a heavy-set man and an attractive blonde woman got out.

'Well?' he demanded as they approached. 'Have you seen the blood tests?'

The woman waved a bee away and nodded. 'Yes, just this morning. Mr Hamilton's done quite a job for us, David. He's a good detective. I thought you might like to meet him.'

The tall man's eyes fixed on the private investigator. 'The blood tests,' he said softly. 'What do they show?'

Hamilton dabbed his face with a handkerchief. 'Jeez, it's hot as hell, isn't it? Nice to meet you, Mr Griffin. I...' His eyes met those of David Griffin and he cleared his throat. 'This was one hell of a tough job,' he said. 'That damned doctor gave me a hard time. We'd agreed on a price and at the last minute he decided to give me a speech on medical ethics. Too late, doc, I told him, you should have thought of that before you agreed to take the money and the kid's blood. You should have...'

David Griffin's eyes darkened. 'Spare me the details, please. What do the tests prove? Is the boy my son or isn't he?'

The private investigator shrugged. 'The blood type's right. And the genetic match-up is damned near perfect.'

David nodded and turned to the woman. 'That's it, then. I'm going to get him tomorrow.'

'David...' The woman, a careful smile on her face, stepped forward. 'Are you sure you want to do this? The repercussions could be horrendous. To suddenly produce a son...'

'The boy is a year old, Vanessa. That's hardly "sudden".'

'You know what I mean, David. You can't just drop this kind of news on the world. There'll be gossip...'

He dismissed her protests with a shrug. 'We've been through all this before. The boy is my responsibility now. His mother's dead and he has no one.'

'He has his aunt, David. She's taking care of him.'

'Oh, that's very reassuring,' he said, his voice heavy with sarcasm. 'When does she take care of him, Vanessa? The report said she spends her nights in a bar and her days sleeping. Isn't that right, Mr Hamilton?'

The detective nodded eagerly. 'Yeah, right. She...'

David Griffin snorted. 'That's a hell of a way to raise my son, isn't it?'

Vanessa Walters took a deep breath and moved closer to him. 'Look,' she said softly, 'I'm not telling you to turn your back on the child. You think he's yours, OK, but...'

'He is mine,' the man said coldly, lifting his face to the sky again. 'The tests prove it.'

'Yes, but... David, you have an image to consider. What will people think?'

His expression softened as the dark speck came into view again. 'Whatever you want them to think,' he said, watching as the hawk circled overhead. 'That's what I pay you for, remember? Figure something out.'

'It isn't that easy, David. The media will eat this stuff up. David Griffin, admitting he's got a year-old son...' She smiled hesitantly and touched his arm. 'We could send the woman money for the child's care.'

His eyes narrowed. 'I'm not asking you for advice, Vanessa.'

'But you pay me to give it,' she answered quickly. 'I wouldn't be doing my job if I didn't tell you how this is going to affect you, especially after all this time. Maybe if you'd acknowledged parentage sooner...'

He waved his hand impatiently. 'Stand back,' he ordered. 'Isis is coming down.' He raised his arm and the others moved away hurriedly as the dark shape hurtled from the sky and settled on his gloved fist in a flurry of feathers, its powerful yellow talons gripping the heavy leather gauntlet. The hawk's golden eyes burned fiercely as she raised her powerful wings and balanced herself with one final muscular beat. 'Easy, girl,' murmured David as he gave her a piece of raw steak. He slipped the leather hood over the hawk's head and Vanessa laughed nervously.

'That creature makes a wreck of me,' she said.

'Ditto,' the detective added with a shudder.

David moved towards the black stallion grazing among the flowers on the hillside. 'I've told you before, there's nothing to be afraid of. Isis is no different from any other predator. She only does what she has to do to survive.' He gathered the stallion's reins in one hand and mounted carefully. 'About the boy,' he said, and the man and the woman stared up at him. 'My mind's made up. He isn't going to grow up without a parent. And he isn't going to be raised by a woman who performs in a bar.'

'She's a waitress, Mr Griffin,' the detective corrected.

'I don't give a damn what she is,' David said sharply, while the stallion snorted and danced nervously beneath him. 'His mother's dead and he has a father. And, as of tomorrow, he's going to know it.' He tapped his heels against the horse's black flanks. 'I'll see you at the office later, Vanessa,' he called, as the horse broke into a canter.

The detective sighed and dug his hands into his pockets. 'Well,' he said, 'I'll—er—I'll send you my bill. It's a little steep, but . . .'

The woman tossed her head impatiently. 'I'll write you a cheque when we get back to the city. I just can't believe he's going to do this. It's so stupid!'

The man shrugged. 'Yeah, well, some people get carried away by emotion. I mean, you wouldn't think a man as tough as David Griffin would admit he's got a bastard son.' The woman looked at him sharply and he flushed. 'Hell,' he said quickly, 'what's so strange about his being as human as the next guy, right? After all, just because the papers call him the Hawk...' His flush deepened, but a broad smile suddenly appeared on her face.

'You've done a wonderful job, Mr Hamilton,' she said briskly. 'Outstanding.'

A slow grin stretched across his features. 'I have?'

Vanessa Walters nodded. 'There'll be a bonus in your cheque,' she said, striding towards the jeep, 'a fat bonus for work well done.'

Hamilton's grin widened. 'Thanks. I told you, Miss Walters, when I do a job, I do it right.'

Laughter trilled in her throat. 'Indeed you do, Mr Hamilton. Indeed you do!'

CHAPTER ONE

RACHEL COOPER blew a lock of dark hair from her face and shifted the bag of groceries in her arms. She grunted as her elbow banged against the doorframe.

'Damn,' she whispered, trying unsuccessfully to balance the bag against her out-thrust hip. A box of disposable nappies was tucked under her other arm and her key, of course, was safely—and impossibly—tucked inside her shoulderbag. Shifting position on the narrow landing outside her apartment, Rachel hoisted the grocery bag higher and aimed her elbow in the general vicinity of the doorbell. It took several efforts, but at last she heard the faint peal of the bell ringing inside the apartment. 'Come on, Mrs Gould, come on,' she muttered. 'Open the darned door...'

The nappy box slipped from beneath her arm just as the door creaked open. Mrs Gould, her white hair in disarray and her face flushed, peered at Rachel.

'Rachel? I thought I heard someone at the door. Here, let me help you with that,' she said, grabbing at the grocery bag. 'You stopped at the all-night market on your way home, I see. Good. We're out of milk... Were you out here long? I must have turned my hearing aid down.'

Rachel smiled through her teeth as she followed after the woman. 'I wish you wouldn't turn it down, Mrs Gould,' she said, lowering her packages to a table in the cramped living-room. 'You won't be able to hear the baby if he cries.'

Mrs Gould's smile faltered. 'I'd never ignore Jamie, Rachel—you know that. I just didn't want to hear the radio from the apartment downstairs. Such awful music! What is this world coming to, I wonder? Don't those young men have jobs? They've been carrying on all night long. Such comings and goings. I was talking to Mrs Greeley this evening and she said...'

Rachel smiled and nodded her head in the pauses of the litany that she assumed were for her response as she took the cold things out of the grocery bag and put them in the refrigerator. Did the old woman spend all her time peering out of the window or gossiping on the phone? It was a question Rachel had wrestled with before. She tried to tell herself it didn't matter; Jamie didn't need much care at night. Rachel put him to bed at six and he was sound asleep by the time Mrs Gould showed up at eight, but it was hard not to wonder what would happen if he became ill or had a nightmare. Don't think that way, Rachel told herself, slamming the refrigerator door shut. Mrs Gould loved the baby. And she charged a reasonable amount for her services. An agency would have provided someone more reliable, but even with the most stringent budgeting, her income couldn't stretch to cover the fee. She sighed and dug into her purse.

'Yes, well, thank you again, Mrs Gould,' she said, turning towards the old woman. 'Let me pay you for this week before you go.'

'You can stop by my apartment later, Rachel,' said Mrs Gould, wrapping a scarf around her shoulders. 'I won't be going until late tomorrow.'

Rachel's brow furrowed. 'Going? Tomorrow? Going where?'

Her neighbour caught her lower lip between her teeth. 'Didn't I tell you? I'm so forgetful lately... My son asked me to stay with him and his wife. She's due any time now, and they've decided against a baby nurse. Why should they go to all that expense when I'm available, I said, and they agreed. I'll call and let you know when I'm coming back.'

Panic sharpened Rachel's voice. 'Yes, but what about Jamie? Who'll take care of him? I won't be able to get anyone in time for tomorrow...'

The old woman shook her head. 'I thought I'd told you, dear—I am sorry. You might ask Mrs Greeley, I suppose... No, she's going to the theatre with her niece. The couple down the hall have a baby-sitter. She's just a child herself, but...'

Rachel nodded wearily. 'I'll work something out. Wish your son and daughter-in-law well for me. And come back as soon as you can.'

Mrs Gould smiled as she opened the front door. 'Of course, Rachel. And you give that boy of yours a hug for me, hmm? Tell him not to forget me while I'm gone.'

Rachel nodded again as she closed the door and leaned her tired body against it. Sometimes she was convinced the only person Jamie was likely to forget was herself. Not that he didn't see her a lot; after all, she was the one who lifted him from his crib each morning, just as she was the one who bathed him and played with him and fed him all day. But it was getting more and more difficult to keep up the pace.

She shrugged free of her coat and kicked off her high-heeled gold sandals. Lord, but they were agony to wear! It was hard enough to have to be on your feet all night, trotting back and forth from the bar to the tables at the Golden Rooster, but to have to do it while wearing four-inch heels was horrible. Usually she changed to sneakers and a sweat-suit after work, but not tonight. There had been a man at one of the tables, a man whose fierce eyes had been on her half the night. He hadn't said anything to her—he'd been someone else's customer—but somehow, the thought of leaving the club alone had made her uneasy, and so she had simply thrown her coat over her costume when one of the other girls offered her a lift home. She winced at she hobbled down the hall towards her bedroom.

'The shoes are killers, I know, but that's what they like, kid,' one of the other cocktail waitresses had told her the first night she'd worked in the Rooster. 'That and these god-awful little skirts that barely cover your rear. Flash 'em enough and you'll double your tips. That's worth it, isn't it?'

Yes, Rachel had thought with a sigh as she counted her tips the end of that first night, yes, it surely was. At this rate, she'd double what she'd been earning as a secretary. And that was all that mattered. Cassie's death had meant more than an emotional wrench; it had meant a loss of income, a big loss. Cassie's modelling fees had been substantial. And raising a child was expensive, especially when you had to pay for someone to care for him...

A smile lit Rachel's face as she entered the bedroom. Jamie lay sprawled in his crib, his little rump raised in the air. She pulled the blanket over him and touched his dark golden curls lightly with her fingers. He was worth everything, she thought, cupping her hand around his head. Tired feet, embarrassing costume, even the customers who thought she was fair game for crude proposals and jokes—her Jamie was worth all that and more. And he was hers; it might have been her stepsister who had carried him and delivered him, but it was Rachel who had walked endless miles at night when the baby had colic, Rachel who had rubbed his sore gums when he cut his first tooth, Rachel who had soothed him and rocked him and loved him...

She jumped at the sound of the doorbell. It was three in the morning. Who could that be? Mrs Gould, with a change of heart about her money? Yes, of course, that would be it. The old woman was growing more and more forgetful lately. She'd probably got all the way up to her apartment and then wondered why Rachel hadn't paid her. Rachel sighed and tiptoed out of the bedroom, quietly closing the door behind her. It was time to do something about replacing Mrs Gould permanently. There had to be a way to get her hands on some extra money. Maybe she could work her days off at the Golden Rooster. Or maybe she could dredge out her old typewriter and do home typing during the day. There were lots of colleges in the New York area; there had to be students who wanted term papers typed or notes transcribed and never mind when she'd find time to do it. She'd make time. She'd...

'Mrs Gould,' she said, as she opened the door. 'I'm glad you came back. I...' The words caught in her throat. There was a man standing in the doorway, the same man who had been watching her all evening. Instinctively, she slammed her hand against the door, but he shouldered it open. 'What do you want? Get away from me!'

'Are you alone, Miss Cooper?'

'Yes,' she said stupidly, then shook her head. 'I mean, no—no, I'm not alone.' Everything she'd ever heard or read about New York flooded into her mind. Jamie, she thought desperately, Jamie... She had to keep him safe. 'Get out of my apartment,' she said, trying to force the door closed. 'I'll scream!'

His smile was thin. 'You'll scream? In a New York City apartment building at this hour of the night? All you'll succeed in doing is waking Jamie, Miss Cooper. And I don't think I'll allow that.'

'Jamie? What do you know about Jamie?'

'Enough to want to continue this conversation inside,' he said.

Rachel looked up into his face. His gold-flecked eyes were fathomless beneath dark brows. Hair that was sun-streaked brown fell over his forehead. He ran his fingers through it and drew it away from his face. And he was big—God, she thought, repressing a shudder, he was huge! Not in height, perhaps, although he was over six feet, but his shoulders were broad. They seemed to fill the doorway. And he had a scar running alongside his mouth. It was faint and small, but it lent him a sinister air that didn't seem to go with his expensively tailored suit. Rachel took a deep breath.

'I'm going to take my chances on screaming,' she said gently. 'You have three seconds to get out of here.'

'Miss Cooper...'

'One one-thousand,' she said.

'Miss Cooper, listen...'

'Two one-thousand, three one-thou...'

'My name is David Griffin, Miss Cooper,' he said brusquely. 'Jamie is my son.'

Rachel felt her legs begin to buckle under her. No, she thought, he couldn't be... But of course he was; she recognised him as soon as he told her his name. Cassie had kept newspaper clippings of him taped to her dressing-table mirror until she'd had the baby, until he had refused to admit he'd fathered her child, until...

'You were at the Golden Rooster tonight,' she whispered.

He nodded. 'I was indeed.'

'Get out!' she snapped. 'You're not welcome here, Mr Griffin. Neither Jamie nor I want to see you.'

He laughed as he brushed past her into the living-room. 'Jamie's a little young to make decisions like that. And I don't give a damn what you want.' He turned and his golden eyes looked past her. 'Your neighbours seem interested, though,' he said politely. 'Good evening.'

Rachel spun around and stared into the hallway at the sleep-befuddled face staring at her from the opposite apartment. Quickly she slammed the door and leaned against it. David Griffin was standing in the centre of the room, smiling coolly at her.

'I'd like to see my son.'

Fury raged through her. 'Your son?' she repeated. 'Just like that? The same son you denied when my sister told you she was pregnant? The same son you denied even after she notified you of his birth?' She lifted her chin and put her hands on her hips. 'Get out, or I'll call the police!'

David Griffin's eyes swept over her. 'You'll forgive me, Miss Cooper. Somehow it's difficult to be intimidated by a woman dressed as you are.' His eyes moved over her again, his glance pausing at the deep V of her black silk shirt, stopping at the black and gold skirt that ended at her thighs. 'As for the police—might I suggest they'd give you more difficulty than they would me?'

Hot colour rushed to Rachel's cheeks. Don't answer him, she told herself. Let him bait you all he likes. Just find out what he wants and get him out of here.

'You want to see your son,' she repeated. 'Why? Why now?'

He looked around the small room, his gaze taking in the shabby furniture, the playpen, the stacks of baby clothes Rachel had not had time to fold during the day. 'I thought of coming by during the day, but I didn't want to run the risk of your being...occupied.'

How had he made such a simple word sound dirty? she wondered. She took a deep breath and forced her eyes to meet his, trying not to think about how exposed her stupid costume made her feel.

'The only thing I'm occupied with during the day is taking care of my baby...'

'Jamie's not your baby. He was Cassie's—and mine. And I want to see him—I already told you that.'

'How touching! You want to see your son. It's a little late, isn't it? Cassie would have given anything to have heard you say those words. Especially after the promises you made her.'

'Promises? What promises?'

'Don't play games with me. You know what you told Cassie.'

David Griffin's lips drew back from his teeth in a mirthless grin. 'The only promise I ever made your sister was that I'd pay her bar bill.'

'She's dead, for God's sake! Can't you admit the truth, even now? You owed her a lot more than that. You...'

'That's what she wanted me to believe, but she was wrong. She...'

Everything that Rachel had wanted to shout in this man's face for months surfaced. David Griffin hadn't seen Cassie's tear-stained face when she told Rachel she was four months pregnant; he hadn't heard Cassie's cries when he'd had his administrative assistant tell her that her phone calls were not welcome; he didn't know the despair of a pregnant woman abandoned by the man who had seduced her. He would never have recognised the Cassie who had come to Rachel in despair more than a year ago, pleading for help, just as she'd always done when they were children. No, all David Griffin would remember was the preening, self-centred cover girl, the Cassie whose face had smiled from a dozen magazine covers. Rachel took a step forward, her embarrassment over her costume forgotten in her anger.

'How dare you come here now? What's the matter, Mr Griffin? Did things get dull for you tonight? Did you suddenly decide to go slumming and see your son? Haven't you got other children you could have visited tonight and just left us alone?'

She gasped with pain as his hands shot forward and grasped her shoulders. Fury roughened his voice. 'That's enough,' he growled. 'Don't say another word!' His eyes darkened, only the golden glints in the brown irises gleamed like fire. Rachel barely breathed; after a moment, he lifted his hands from her shoulders with exaggerated care and dropped them to his sides. 'I am here precisely because I would never desert a child of mine,' he said carefully. 'While Cassie was alive, I admit, I didn't believe the boy belonged to me. But then I read of her death...' He ran his hand through his hair and turned away. 'Is this how you live?' he asked, looking around the cramped room. 'You and the boy?'

The hair rose on Rachel's arms. Somebody was walking on her grave, her grandmother used to say at such moments, and that was how she felt now, as if something terrible was about to happen. 'There's nothing wrong with how we live,' she said quickly, moving towards the couch. Unconsciously, she snatched up some of Jamie's clothing and began to fold it. 'I admit, it's small, but it was the best I could do after Cassie died. Look, why don't you go? You wanted to satisfy your curiosity, and you have. I'll... I'll send you a photo of Jamie...'

David Griffin took a deep breath. 'It's not curiosity that brought me here,' he said finally. 'I came because of my son.'

'A minute ago he wasn't your son,' she said, picking up the stack of baby clothes and holding them to her chest. 'I told you, I'll send you a picture.'

'He is my son,' he said flatly. 'I've seen his birth certificate. I'm entered as his father.'

'How? I have the certificate. I...'

'And I've had blood tests done. The boy is mine, Miss Cooper. I'm positive of it.'

'Blood tests? But...but...' Dear God, she thought, money and power could buy anything. Last week the doctor had taken a blood sample, to test for allergies, he'd said. And she'd believed him. She'd believed him... 'What is it you want?' she whispered. 'Now that Cassie's dead, what's the difference?'

David sank down on the couch and stretched his legs out in front of him. There was a sudden weariness in his face.

'It's Cassie's death that's made the difference. When I heard she'd died of drugs...'

'She didn't know what she was doing...'

'...when she died, I began to wonder about the boy. He had no father; now, he has no mother.'

'He has me,' Rachel said quickly, her voice sounding breathless. 'He's always had me.'

'Indeed,' said David, his gaze moving over her again until she felt naked under the hard, golden stare. 'You and an old woman who can't even remember her own name half the time.'

'Mrs Gould loves Jamie. And I'm thinking of getting someone else...'

His lips pulled back from his teeth. 'What are you going to pay them with, Miss Cooper? Free drinks at your club?'

A flush darkened her cheeks. 'I'm not ashamed of my job, Mr Griffin. It's honest work and it supports us.'

'Look, this is useless,' he said, getting to his feet. 'There's no easy way to tell you this.' His eyes met Rachel's and she thought she saw pity in their golden depths, then his expression hardened. 'I've come for my son. I'm taking him home.'

'You're *what*?' Rachel's voice rose an octave. 'Are you crazy?' she demanded. 'This is his home. You can't just walk in here and...' Jamie's thin wail cut through her words. 'Now see what you've done,' she snapped furiously. 'You've awakened my baby!' She turned and hurried to the closed bedroom door. David hesitated for an instant and then followed after her. 'It's all right, sweetheart,' she crooned as she opened the door. 'It's all right. I'm here, Jamie, I'm here.'

The child's voice was ragged with relief. 'Mama?' he sobbed.

Rachel switched on the night light and then bent over the crib. David watched as the crying child within lifted his arms to her. My eyes, he thought with a shock of recognition, while she swooped the baby into her embrace, he has my eyes... Jamie hiccuped softly and Rachel rubbed his back while she cuddled him against her breast. Finally the child's sobs stopped. He gave David a sleepy, curious glance, then his head dropped against Rachel's shoulder. She turned towards David, her eyes pleading with him.

'He's asleep,' she whispered. 'Please, wait for me in the living-room.'

David's eyes were riveted on Jamie. It seemed an eternity before he nodded his head.

'All right,' he said gruffly, 'I'll be in the next room.'

She waited until the door closed behind him. Then, carefully, she laid the sleeping child back in the crib and drew the cover over him.

'Don't you worry,' she whispered, stroking his cheek. 'I won't let anyone take you from me, Jamie, you'll see. We'll be fine as long as we have each other.'

She took a deep breath and switched out the light. David Griffin had appeared out of nowhere and he'd go back to nowhere just as quickly. Wasn't possession nine-tenths of the law? Jamie was hers, not anybody else's. Squaring her shoulders, Rachel stepped into the living-room.

'Mr Griffin, I appreciate your concern,' she began, 'but it's misplaced. Jamie's been doing just fine without you...'

'He'll do a hell of a lot better with me.'

'I don't think you understand,' she said carefully. 'I have custody of him. I'm his aunt.'

'You have possession, Miss Cooper,' he said coldly. 'And you're not even a blood relative. You and Cassie were stepsisters.'

'I love him,' said Rachel, hating the way her voice trembled.

'Jamie is my son. Nothing you can say or do can alter that fact.'

'And he loves me,' she said, as if David hadn't spoken. A tremor raced through her and she wrapped her arms around herself. 'Have you thought about that? He loves me. He...he thinks I'm his mother...'

'Yes,' David said unpleasantly, 'I noticed.'

'It must be wonderful to have the money to buy everything you want,' she said, fighting against the quiver in her voice. 'But you'll never be able to buy that baby's love. Never. He doesn't even know you...' She swallowed and took a breath. 'Look,' she said slowly, 'we can work something out. I won't object if you want to see your...want to see Jamie. I...I'd even understand if you wanted to take him out for the day...' A faint smile flickered at the corners of David's mouth and Rachel plunged on with hope born of desperation. 'You could do that, you know, you could even have him for a weekend once in a while, when he's older... Damn you, David Griffin, why are you laughing?'

'Are you sure you and Cassie were only stepsisters? That's pretty good, Miss Cooper. Cassie laid a neat little scheme to con me into marriage and I managed to side-step it—and now here you are, offering me what sounds a hell of a lot like the kind of visitation rights a divorced father gets from his wife. Maybe you'd let me send the boy some support money too. Wouldn't that be nice, eh?' The smile vanished from his face and he took a quick step forward. Despite herself, Rachel stumbled back. 'I don't know what your game is, Rachel,' he said softly. 'Maybe you really care for the child. Maybe he fills some kind of emptiness inside you.' He moved forward again, until only inches separated them. 'Or are you like Cassie?' he asked in an ominous voice. 'Do you bring men here where my son can see what you do?'

Rachel shook her head wildly. 'I don't know what you're talking about,' she whispered. 'I'm a cocktail waitress, I told you that. I . . .'

'It's a touching story,' growled David. 'And you do it all for Jamie.'

'Yes,' she said, 'for the money . . .'

His hand closed around the dark spill of her hair. 'I'll bet it's for the money,' he murmured, drawing her towards him. 'Just like Cassie . . .'

His mouth came down on hers, covering it with a cruel passion. She cried out against his lips, but he was too strong, too certain of what he believed. Rachel's eyes filled with tears. They crept down her cheeks as she stood rigid in his unyielding embrace. His hand spread in the tangle of her hair and he cupped the back of her head. For the span of a heartbeat her mouth trembled beneath his, then she put her hands against his chest and pushed free of his punishing embrace.

'Let go of me!' You're everything Cassie said you were!'

The golden eyes flashed darkly. 'Cassie didn't know a damned thing about me.'

'She knew you didn't want her baby.'

His lips twisted in a parody of a smile. 'She was right, Rachel. But I want mine. And he's not going to stay here another night.'

She shook her head in disbelief. 'No, please ... That's cruel!'

His hands fell to his sides and he laughed. 'Cruel? To acknowledge the boy as my son and heir? To take him to my home and give him everything money can buy? Is that your definition of cruelty, Rachel?'

'But you don't ... you don't want him ... You don't know him ... He doesn't like cold milk—you don't even know that. You don't know that he has bad dreams unless you leave the door open while he's falling asleep. You don't know that he loves Jack and the Beanstalk but he cries if you read him Little Red Riding Hood ...'

She caught her lip between her teeth. What was she doing? She could hear the desperation in her voice. She sounded pathetic. Jamie's idiosyncrasies wouldn't matter to a man like this, a man whose money and power could buy everything. There had to be a way to reach him, a way to stop him destroying her and Jamie. Think of something, she told herself furiously. Think, damn you, Rachel Cooper, think!

'You can't get away with something like this,' she said with more conviction than she felt. 'No court would take him from me.'

'No court would hesitate. My lawyers have assured me of that.'

'You can't just steal him from me! I'll ... I'll go to the newspapers. I'll tell them about you. I'll ...'

'You'd have to tell them about Cassie, too,' he said softly. 'Have you thought about that?'

'I don't care,' she said, desperation in her voice. 'I'll do whatever I must. Jamie needs me. He'll be lost without me. He ...'

Suddenly he nodded his head. 'All right, Rachel, you've made your point. Jamie and I don't know each other yet, and I don't want to make this any harder for him than it must be. You can come with him. I'll hire you as Jamie's nursemaid.'

No, she thought, this was his idea of a joke...

David paused and then nodded again. 'Yes, that's what we'll do.' A smile touched his lips. 'You can stay with him for a while.'

'A while?' she repeated in disbelief.

David shrugged his shoulders. 'Until he can adapt to someone who's better qualified to care for him. And then I'll give you a substantial bonus and...'

'You can't buy me off,' she said bitterly, 'just as you couldn't buy Cassie off.'

He shrugged impatiently. 'Take it or leave it,' he said, glancing at his watch. 'I have an important appointment tomorrow and I've got to get some sleep tonight. Are you going to take my offer or aren't you? The choice is yours.'

The choice is mine, she thought, staring at his expressionless face. But David Griffin had made the choice for her, just as he had made it for Cassie.

'Yes,' she murmured, hating herself for being so powerless, 'yes, I'll accept your offer.'

'Good,' he said, patting her shoulder. 'You won't regret it.'

But you will, she thought, repressing a shudder as his hand touched her. You will.

CHAPTER TWO

'WE'LL be at the house soon. Is there anything you want my housekeeper to make ready for the child?'

Rachel turned at the sound of David Griffin's voice. The emotionless words were the first he had spoken during the past two hours as they drove up the Hudson River towards the darkly looming Catskill Mountains. She turned towards him, watching as he reached towards the car telephone beneath the dashboard. Jamie stirred in her arms and sighed in his sleep.

'Nothing, thank you,' she said with curt formality. 'I have everything I need.'

David glanced at her. 'Shall I call her and ask her to prepare some breakfast?'

'Breakfast? At this hour?' She shook her head. 'All Jamie will want is his bottle. And you don't have to bother her on my account.'

'I won't be bothering her, Rachel. I've told her to be waiting for us when we arrive.'

And she'll do your bidding, Rachel thought. She's in your employ, just as I am. She turned away from his impassive profile and stared blindly out the window of the luxurious BMW sedan. At least there was some comfort in knowing there was a housekeeper waiting for them. They were driving along roads so isolated that she had felt they were leaving civilisation behind. There hadn't been time to tell anyone that she'd gone with this man, not that there was anyone to tell, really. Her parents had been dead for eight years, ever since her eighteenth summer. And her grandmother was only a childhood memory. Mrs Gould, perhaps, but she was going off to visit her son. The owner of the Golden Rooster would grumble for an evening and then replace her with another girl. David Griffin hadn't given her the time to do anything except pack a small suitcase. He'd stationed himself at the doorway of her tiny living-room and glanced at his watch.

'You have half an hour,' he'd said. 'Just take what you and the child will need for the day. One of my people will come in and pack the rest of your things.'

It was an order, not a suggestion. Anger blossomed within her like a hot white flower, but she forced it away. Don't antagonise him, she warned herself. He could just as easily change his mind and take Jamie away without her. She was forced to do as she'd been told.

His eyes were on her as she pulled a suitcase from the closet, and she packed without conscious thought, her hands and body functioning automatically while her mind remained detached, racing in ever-tightening circles, searching for a way out of this nightmare. But there was none that she could see. 'The Hawk', the papers called him, a predator who swooped down on defenceless corporations and carried them off. He did the same with women, Cassie had said, although they were easier prey than the corporations. If David Griffin set out to seduce a woman, she was going to be his. He was too charming, too sensual, too...

Rachel had glanced at him as she packed. There was nothing charming about him now. His mouth was drawn into a cruel line, and his eyes were cold and hooded. The Hawk indeed! she thought, cramming things into her suitcase. And she and Jamie were certainly defenceless, although why he'd chosen to come into their lives was a mystery. He was here because Jamie needed a father, he'd said, but the boy had needed a father long before Cassie's death.

'Aren't you finished yet?' he asked impatiently. 'I told you to hurry.'

Rachel slammed the suitcase closed and turned to face him. 'I know what you told me,' she snapped. 'Would you like me to click my heels and salute too?'

His smile was cold. 'Perhaps you'd prefer not to accompany the child, Rachel. That can be arranged.'

That's it, Rachel, she thought as her heart began to race. Make him change his mind about letting you go with Jamie. That'll be marvellous, won't it? She turned away from his empty stare and swallowed the angry words that filled her mouth. Everything had happened too suddenly. She needed time to think, time to plan. And there would be time, if only she didn't let rage make her say or do something stupid. Carefully she walked past him to the bedroom, turning on the lamp nearest the door. Jamie stirred almost immediately and began to cry. Rachel bent over the crib and lifted him into her arms, cuddling his sleep-warmed body against her.

'It's all right,' she whispered, and then David had stepped into the room.

'Give the boy to me and finish your packing.'

She had turned towards him, watching as his golden eyes focused on the baby. Reluctantly, she had handed over the drowsing child. He had accepted Jamie awkwardly, holding him as if he were made of glass. Then, to her surprise, his tense features softened and he smiled down at the baby. The child frowned and Rachel stepped forward, anticipating a loud wail. But Jamie's frown changed to a smile. Pain had lanced through her as she looked from the man to the baby. You didn't need birth certificates or blood tests or Cassie's rambling story to prove these two were father and son. There was the same darkly waving hair, the same wide, gold-flecked eyes, the same full lower lip.

The sound of the car changing down on the steep mountain grade brought her back to the present. She glanced at the man beside her. It was hard to picture Cassie with him. Cassie had liked men who were wealthy, yes, and powerful—those qualities had been all too attractive to her. But she had preferred men who laughed and joked a lot, men who would do nothing but dance attendance on her. It was hard to envisage this man dancing attendance on any woman. But her stepsister had told her about David's determined seduction, about the flowers and phone calls and promises that had lured her into his bed for a long Caribbean weekend.

Her eyes moved over David's face, visible in the pale dawn light. There was a grim set to his mouth, a hardness to his jawline, but even so, a hint of sensuality lurked beneath the cold exterior. He wasn't the type Cassie had usually liked. She had preferred her men fair and polished, but there was nothing polished about this man. He was rough and abrasively masculine, in spite of his well-tailored three-piece suit. Rachel could see the faint scar she had noticed earlier, and now, seeing him in profile, she realised that his nose was slightly crooked, as if it had once been broken and improperly healed. He had high cheekbones and a faintly clefted square jaw. His lashes were long and sooty over those strange, gold-flecked eyes that had seemed to look through her hours before.

Her glance drifted to his hands lying loosely on the steering wheel, the fingers long and lean. She could still remember their bite as he'd pulled her into his arms and punished her with a kiss that told her, more clearly than words, what he thought of her. What had he judged her by? she wondered. The way she looked in her Golden Rooster costume? She glanced down at her old corduroy trousers and shapeless sweater. This was the real Rachel Cooper, not the woman who wore black net stockings and four-inch-high heels. 'Don't judge a book by its cover,' had been another of her grandmother's sayings, and it was a good one. She was still the same person she'd been when she was a secretary and wore dark dresses and suits. The only difference was that she earned more money now, money she needed to support a child. And being a cocktail waitress meant she had the daylight hours free to be with Jamie. Her life was hard, but Jamie made it all worthwhile. He was worth everything. He...

'I should think the boy would be too much for you,' David said suddenly.

Was the man a mind-reader? Rachel wondered. Her eyes met his defiantly. 'He's never been too much for me.'

A thin smile tilted the corner of his mouth. 'We'll get along better if you don't read a hidden message into everything I say, Rachel. I only meant that he seems quite an armful, and I had a special seat installed for him in the back.'

She barely glanced into the shadowed rear of the BMW. 'Yes, so I noticed. You were sure of the outcome, weren't you, Mr Griffin? You never doubted that you'd get your own way, did you?'

'This isn't a contest of wills, Rachel. Jamie is my son. I have legal rights.'

Rachel swallowed past the bitter taste that flooded her mouth. 'You don't have to keep reminding me of that,' she said flatly. 'That's the only reason Jamie and I are here. Believe me, if I thought for a minute I could fight your money and your lawyers and your name...'

He looked at her again. The lightening sky allowed her to see the faint gleam of amusement in his eyes.

'Tell yourself that, if it makes it easier. But you and I will get along better once you accept the facts.'

Her anger overrode her caution at the smug assurance in his voice. 'You and I won't get along at all! Cassie told me exactly what kind of man you were, and she was right. You...' She bit back the rest of her words and turned away from him.

'Don't stop now,' he said in a silky voice. 'So few people have the courage to tell me what they think of me to my face.'

'How on earth my sister could have become involved with someone like you...'

'I suppose I'm everything Cassie said I was.'

Her eyes met his. 'You are indeed. My sister...'

'Your stepsister.'

Rachel shrugged impatiently. 'I never thought of her as anything but my sister. My father married her mother when she was four and I was eight. I took care of her and advised her...'

David smiled mirthlessly. 'Not very well.'

A flush rose to her cheeks. 'Cassie didn't ask my advice about you, unfortunately. She was a grown woman— but I wish I'd known how you were pressuring her. I'd have tried to talk her out of going away with you.'

He laughed. 'Is that what she told you?'

'Are you surprised? We were very close. She told me everything—how you treated her when she found out she was pregnant, how you denied the child she was carrying was yours. It's too bad it took her death to change your mind,' she added, bitterness sharpening her voice. 'It's a little late for Cassie.'

'My concern is for my son,' he said coldly. 'Nothing more.'

'I really wish I could find that touching, Mr Griffin. But somehow all this concern seems out of character. I just don't see you as the fatherly type. This sudden interest in Jamie puzzles me. I don't understand...'

'You don't have to,' he said bluntly. 'All you have to do is make the transition period easier for him. After he's made the adjustment, I'll keep my end of the bargain. I'll pay you handsomely. I may even agree to let you see the boy once in a great while.'

The breath caught in her throat as she pictured the loneliness of a future without Jamie. 'Once in a while?' she repeated.

David nodded. 'And I'll keep my word. I've been told that's my greatest asset.'

Rachel's eyebrows rose. 'Well,' she said evenly, 'one asset is better than none.'

She grasped the arm-rest as the car whipped around a narrow curve. They were climbing a ribbon of road that circled around a mountain in smaller and smaller rings. Suddenly the grey stone walls of a house became visible through the trees, glowering over a meadow like a prehistoric beast.

'Is that your house?'

The car slowed before an iron gate that was overgrown with ivy. David nodded and pressed a button on the dash. 'My home,' he said, while the gate slowly opened. 'And Jamie's.'

The way he said it seemed designed to remind her of her status as Jamie's nurse, but it was unnecessary. The enormous house looming before them was as intimidating as its owner and sufficient reminder that she was only an employee. Rachel shifted uneasily, clutching the sleeping child more closely to her as they drove into the circular driveway and stopped before the front door. He switched off the engine just as the door swung open, and a middle-aged couple emerged from the house. Rachel half expected the man to open the car door, but he stood back, smiling politely, while David let himself out of the BMW.

'Good morning, Barton. The car's stumbling a bit. Check the injectors, will you?'

'Yes, sir. How'd she handle otherwise?'

David grinned, and the hard lines of his face softened as they had when he'd held Jamie in his arms.

'Like a kestrel aching to try her wings,' he said.

The man smiled. 'Then I'll check those injectors right away.' He glanced at Rachel and nodded. 'Morning, ma'am. Nice to meet you.'

Rachel nodded stiffly. They hadn't met, not really, but this man—the chauffeur or the butler, it seemed—didn't seem the least surprised at the sight of a slightly dishevelled woman with a baby in her arms. Well, she thought, of course—David Griffin had said his house-keeper had been alerted. The woman probably had told the servants—and there would be servants, many of them, she thought uncomfortably, looking at the house again. And she...she was one of them now.

'Barton will put your things in your room,' said David as she stepped from the car. 'This is Emma, my house-keeper. Give the boy to her.'

Another command, Rachel thought. 'I can manage.'

'I didn't ask if you could manage, Rachel.'

'I know you didn't,' she said carefully. 'I'm simply telling you that I can. I have been, all along...'

'Give him to her!'

His voice snapped like a whip. She lifted her chin and stared into his eyes. *Don't anger him,* a voice inside her whispered, but the contempt she read in them made her spine stiffen.

'No,' she said. The simple word hung in the air between them.

His eyes narrowed. 'Emma,' he said softly, and the housekeeper stepped forward, wiping her hands on her apron.

'You can trust me, miss,' she said. 'The lad will be fine.'

Rachel looked into the woman's smiling face and then she sighed. 'He's probably hungry,' she said.

Emma nodded. 'I raised five of my own,' she said as
Rachel put the sleeping child into her outstretched arms.
'Ah, he's a beautiful child, isn't he?'

'Take him to the nursery,' David said sharply. 'Rachel,
give Emma Jamie's things.'

It was useless to argue. A lump rose in her throat as
she handed the suitcase over. She felt as if she were re-
linquishing Jamie for ever, and she was. This was, after
all, the beginning of his life as David Griffin's son.

'He needs changing...' she began, and David's hand
closed on her shoulder.

'Emma is quite capable. After we settle some things,
you can join him.' His eyes followed hers and he laughed
sharply. 'The house isn't going to swallow him. Believe
me, you'll have no trouble finding the nursery.'

He was making fun of her, she knew that—but there
was an underlying truth in the jest. The house was huge.
It wasn't difficult to imagine endless corridors and rooms
opening into other rooms, all of it like a gloomy labyr-
inth. Taking a breath, she followed him through the door,
readying herself for an interior as cold and forbidding
as its owner. Her apartment was shabby and tiny, but
at least it had a warmth this place would never achieve.

She stumbled to a surprised halt as the door swung
shut behind her. Instead of the dark Victorian gloom
and lumpy velvet furnishings she had expected, the entry
foyer was all light woods and smoked glass. There were
pots and tubs of plants everywhere. There was even a
small tree just beside the door, its oval leaves silvery green
in the early morning sun that illuminated the room
through a huge skylight. A pale blue Aubusson runner
led across the parquet floor towards a curving staircase
that climbed to the second-floor balcony. A door
slammed shut somewhere overhead, and Rachel tilted
her head back, trying unsuccessfully to catch a glimpse

of the housekeeper. David took her by the elbow and led her through the foyer and past the stairs.

'I assure you, he'll be fine. I'm going to arrange for some breakfast. Are you sure you won't have something?'

'No,' she said automatically, although this time the offer made her stomach growl. When had she eaten last? Before she went to work? No, no, she'd been running late... And there hadn't even been time to snatch a sandwich at the club. It had been a busy night, and one of the other waitresses hadn't shown up. The rest of them had had to work their tails off. But she couldn't bring herself to accept anything from David Griffin. Her stomach growled again and she cleared her throat to cover the sound. 'Coffee, perhaps,' she said at last.

He nodded. 'Fine. We'll have it in the library while we talk.'

He motioned towards a closed door. Rachel watched as he started down the hall, his footsteps muffled by the Aubusson. That was pathetic, she thought, as her stomach grumbled again. A lot she'd prove by not eating. Hunger strikes were meaningful for political prisoners, but not for her. After all, she wouldn't help Jamie if she fell flat on her face or got sick. *Call him back and tell him you'll take some toast with the coffee, at least...*

No, she thought, pressing her lips together, no, she'd take nothing from David Griffin. Not a damned thing. The housekeeper—Emma—had seemed friendly enough. Later, after she and Griffin had finished their 'talk', she'd ask the woman for some coffee and toast. Wait in the library, he'd said, as if she were a servant to order around. But that was precisely what she was going to be, wasn't she? David Griffin's servant. His employee. His property. Their 'talk' was probably going to be a series of house rules and restrictions.

Don't think that way, she told herself grimly, walking quickly to the closed door. Don't let him intimidate you. All that matters is staying with Jamie.

She stepped into the library and the door swung shut behind her. Shadows darkened the corners of the large, gloomy room. So much for first impressions, Rachel thought, looking around her. Apparently the airy lightness of the entry foyer did not extend to the rest of the house. There were no light woods, no glass, no Aubusson rugs here. And there were no books, either, even though he'd called the room a library. The walls were lined with tapestries that were pale and faded with age, filled with men on horseback and strange birds with great, curving beaks and fierce eyes. There was a strange smell in the air—not unpleasant exactly, Rachel thought, wrinkling her nose, but not like anything she'd come across before.

She moved slowly towards the nearest tapestry-covered wall. A bird—an eagle, she thought—stared out at her in profile, its oval eye filled with an impersonal rage. There was some soft, furry thing held in its taloned foot. Rachel shuddered and moved on, sniffing at the air again. The strange odour was stronger. What was it? Sharp, acidic—maybe it was just as well she hadn't asked for breakfast. Did the entire house smell this way? Her stomach knotted in rebellion.

Something rustled drily and Rachel's heart thumped against her ribs. Over there, in the corner, behind an ornate wooden screen, something was moving. She took a deep breath. Stop it! she thought fiercely. This was not a Gothic novel. These were not the English moors and she was not a swooning governess. A nervous laugh bubbled up in her throat. *But you're doing a pretty fair job of pretending to be one,* was the unbidden response. The noise came again, papery and somehow alien. A mouse, she thought, moving towards the screen. A house this old was probably mouse heaven. Although it sounded awfully big for a mouse. And the smell was stronger. A rat? Could that be it? An involuntary shudder shook her. Mice were one thing; rats were quite another.

'Come on, Rachel,' she said aloud, 'stop being a fool. Just step up to the screen and...'

She heard the door swing open and then David's voice was sharp behind her. 'Stop, Rachel! Dammit, don't...'

More orders, she thought. More intimidation. Well, it wouldn't work. She was made of tougher stuff. And she wasn't about to click her heels and salute every time he barked out a command. She...

And then everything was happening in slow motion, like a dream from which she could not escape. She walked into something; it was soft and hot, and suddenly a creature from hell launched itself at her face, a thing with a serpentine neck and eyes that blazed with omnipotent fury, a thing with wings and claws. The acidic smell was in her nostrils. She gagged and threw her hands in the air, in front of her face, but not before she'd seen the blood on the thing's breast—and then there was blood on her hands, blood on her sweater, and her screams and the screams of the creature were the same, high and thin and piercing. She stumbled backwards, flailing at it, trying to drive it away.

'Stop it, Isis,' a voice growled, 'get the hell away!' Rachel turned blindly towards the voice, and suddenly strong arms closed securely around her. 'Are you all right? Rachel...'

She shook her head, burying her face against David's chest. 'David,' she gasped, 'thank God—that thing tried to kill me...' She burrowed tightly into the curve of his arm while one of his hands stroked her back.

'No,' he murmured, 'no, she didn't. You frightened her.'

Rachel tilted her head back and stared into his face. 'I frightened her? That creature...'

'Isis,' he said. 'She's a goshawk and her name is Isis.'

'I don't care what she is! She attacked me—I'm bleeding! My hands...'

His fingers closed around her wrists and he lifted her hands, turning them carefully. 'You're not bleeding,' he said. 'You're fine.'

Rachel shook her head. 'There's blood all over me,' she insisted.

'There's only a smear on your sweater, Rachel. Isis was eating.' His hands pressed against her shoulders. 'Take a look at her perch. There's a piece of meat lying on it. That's what the blood is from.'

She forced herself to look past him. The goshawk stared back at her with fierce yellow eyes. One taloned foot rested on a chunk of bloody, raw steak. Rachel shuddered and shook her head.

'A thing like that doesn't belong in a house,' she said. 'It should be outdoors, where it can't attack people.'

David's eyebrows rose. 'She didn't attack you, Rachel. You stumbled into her perch. She was only defending herself. If you'd calm down... What the hell were you doing in here? I told you to wait for me in the library.'

'That's right, try to make it sound as if I'm to blame!' she snapped, pulling free of his arms. 'You told me to wait here.'

David shook his head. 'I told you to go into the library.'

'Stop playing word games, will you!' she snapped furiously. 'You pointed to this room. I don't care if it's the library or not. If you're going to keep something that dangerous in here, it should be behind a locked door. What if Jamie had come into this room instead of me? What if that...that thing had bitten him?'

'Somehow I have difficulty picturing a one-year-old child reaching the doorknob and forcing his way in here, Rachel.'

'Are you suggesting that I did? And that's not the point, anyway. I . . .'

'And the hawk didn't bite you. She didn't do anything to you, as a matter of fact.' He turned towards the goshawk and ran his hand lightly along her pale grey breast. 'Isn't that right, girl?' he asked softly. The hawk shook herself and her feathers rose in a silvery froth. 'Easy, Isis, don't be upset. You're fine.'

The man was insane, Rachel thought, watching him as he stroked the goshawk. Either that, or she was. But one thing was certain: David Griffin might have all the money and power in the world, but he would never have Jamie. There wasn't a way in the world she would let the baby stay in this house, not for another minute. She ran her hands along her sweater, shuddering as she brushed away a drift of soft grey feathers, then she took a deep breath.

'All right, Mr Griffin,' she said softly, 'this game is over. You took me by surprise this morning—of course, you must have planned on that. It was a good ploy, I must admit. Showing up without warning, at that hour . . . but I've come to my senses now.' He turned and looked at her, and the expression of uninterest on his face enraged her. It was the way she sometimes looked at Jamie at the end of a long day, when his infantile babbling was amusing but not really very important. 'I know you think you hold all the cards,' she said, fighting to control her temper, 'and I admit you almost had me believing it too. But there are child welfare laws in this state, and not even someone like you can ignore them. Keeping a wild animal in the house isn't legal . . .'

His smile was cold. 'Ah, that's good to know, Rachel. You're not just a barmaid, you're also a lawyer. That's reassuring. I must tell my attorneys to consult with you in future.'

Her hands trembled with the desire to strike him. Stay calm, she told herself. Just stay calm...

'I am leaving,' she said softly. 'And I'm taking Jamie with me. You'll have to get a court order if you want him. And when we get to court, I'll tell the judge about your...your hawk and... Dammit,' she hissed, 'this isn't funny! What are you smiling at?'

David shook his head. 'I was just picturing you trying to explain yourself out of being arrested for kidnapping, that's all.'

Her face flushed with indignation. 'Kidnapping? That's impossible.'

His face darkened. 'Of course it is. You'd have to get past me first.' He took a step forward and, instinctively, she shrank back.

'It...it isn't kidnapping to try and protect a child,' she said quickly. 'That hawk...'

'It's quite legal to keep and fly a goshawk in this state. Falconry is an ancient and honourable sport. I wouldn't expect you to know that, of course—I'm sure it's not one of the things people talk about at the Golden Rooster.'

Rage flooded her mouth with the taste of copper. She had never despised anyone as she despised this man. And she was powerless before him. How in heaven's name could Cassie have fallen under his spell? It made more sense to think of Jack the Ripper as a charmer. Rachel stared at him in silence, the only sound in the room the raggedness of her own breathing and the papery rustle of the bird's feathers as it settled itself on the perch. Finally she nodded her head.

'You win,' she said in a harsh whisper. 'But the hawk goes. She doesn't belong in the house when there's a child in it.' David started to speak, and she raised her hand to silence him. 'I don't care if you're King Midas himself,' she said quietly, her eyes boring into his, 'I'll bring the law down on you for endangering the welfare of a minor, if I have to.'

She held her breath. It was a bluff—she couldn't picture herself or anyone else doing anything David Griffin didn't want done. For a second she thought she'd pushed him too far. Something flashed in his eyes, and then it was gone. He nodded.

'Fine,' he said mildly. 'Isis was only here temporarily, anyway. She was hurt last week and I've been keeping her indoors so I could watch her. But she's much better now. I'll take her outside.' He glanced at his watch and then his fingers closed around Rachel's arm. 'It's getting late. Emma will show you to your room so you can wash and then I want you to join me for breakfast. You won't have any trouble finding the library this time, I hope.'

'No trouble at all,' she said stiffly, deliberately refusing to acknowledge the sarcastic barb. Pulling free of his hand, she moved quickly towards the door. Her hand was on the knob when she felt a strange sensation between her shoulders. She turned her head and saw that the goshawk's great eyes were on her, burning and fierce. 'The hawk,' she said slowly, 'Isis... You said she'd been hurt. What happened to her?'

His answer was brief and taut. 'Someone shot her.'

'You mean that's how you got her? She'd been wounded and you found her on your property?'

He shook his head. 'Isis was mine to begin with. In a way, it's my fault she was hurt. I was the one who taught her to trust people.'

Rachel stared at him, waiting for him to say something more, but he simply opened the door and waited for her to step into the corridor. 'And?' she asked finally. 'What happened?'

'I was flying her near the edge of my property, and a fool with a gun shot her, wounded her. She barely managed to get back.'

Her eyes met his. 'And? What happened to him? The man who shot your hawk, I mean?'

His eyes turned to ice. 'What do you think happened to him, Rachel? He'll never shoot another hawk, that's for sure. I take care of my own in my own way.'

A shudder ran through her and she looked back at the goshawk. She had seen eyes like those before. They were in David Griffin's face.

CHAPTER THREE

RACHEL awoke abruptly, sitting upright in bed with the covers clutched to her breast, her heart pulsing in her throat. She had been dreaming about Jamie, about coming home from a long night at the Golden Rooster and finding his crib empty, the apartment empty...

She lay back against the pillows and took a deep breath. Nights at the Rooster were behind her now. So was the apartment. She was here, in this house high on a mountain overlooking the Hudson River, but she would be here only so long as David Griffin permitted it. She ran her hand across her forehead, pushing her hair back from her face. The dark hours of the endless night had finally given way and daylight streamed through french doors, illuminating her room. It was handsomely furnished, but it lacked the only thing that mattered. Jamie wasn't sharing the room with her; he was next door, in a room adjoining hers, by order of David Griffin.

Rachel tossed the silk quilt aside and swung her feet to the floor. Everything in this gilded prison was by order of David Griffin, she thought, looking about her. There might as well have been bars separating her from Jamie.

'I want him to start getting used to this house,' David had said the day before. 'And I want him to become used to other people.'

'But he's never spent the night alone,' Rachel had said quickly. 'He's always had Mrs Gould or me...'

'He won't be alone. I've had an intercom installed in the nursery. Emma will be able to hear every sound he makes.'

'Emma? Emma doesn't know anything about him.'

'She'll learn,' he'd said in tones rough with impatience.

'He wakes for a bottle at six in the morning. How will she learn that? He can't tell her. He...'

David had risen from the table, tossing his linen napkin aside with abrupt finality. 'You'll tell her, Rachel. That's why you're here.'

'But...'

'That's the end of it,' he'd said, his eyes flashing a warning. 'There's nothing further to discuss.'

Rachel sighed as she padded barefoot across the room. That was how all her protests had ended. 'There's nothing further to discuss,' David Griffin said whenever she objected to something. And always, implicit in the statement, was a reminder of her transiency in this house. And so she had swallowed her protests and nodded in agreement, all too aware of how readily he could eliminate her from his plans.

She opened the connecting door and looked into the gaily decorated nursery. Empty, she thought without much surprise. Jamie must be downstairs, eating the oatmeal and banana she'd told Emma he liked. So far, the baby had liked everything, she thought grimly, including the roomful of stuffed animals and the wooden mobile over his crib and...

'Stop the self-pity, Rachel,' she said aloud, marching back into her bedroom. 'It won't change things.'

She pulled yesterday's baggy corduroys and shapeless sweater from the chair where she'd dropped them. The million-dollar question, of course, was what *would* change things? Sighing, she slipped the sweater over her head. She'd spent most of the night trying to come up with an answer, but there didn't seem to be any. All that kept dancing through her head was another of Grandma's old sayings: 'Be grateful for small favours'.

'I am grateful,' Rachel whispered, as if her dead grandmother could hear her. After all, she was here, in the Griffin house, and that in itself was surprising when you came right down to it, Rachel thought, zipping up her cords. Hadn't the man been ready to snatch Jamie up and carry him off without any thought for her? Why, it hadn't even occurred to him that Jamie might have trouble adjusting to a new life until she'd suggested it...

Rachel pulled on her socks and her sneakers. Time to be grateful again, she thought, remembering how readily he had agreed to her suggestion that he take her along. Amazing, considering how much he obviously disliked her. Her fingers slowed as she tied the sneaker laces. 'Don't look a gift horse in the mouth,' Grandma probably would have said, but the Trojans hadn't, and look what had happened to them.

She sighed and got to her feet. 'Never mind all that, Rachel,' she muttered aloud. 'Just get down there and show that...that chunk of ice that you're indispensable. Convince him that Jamie can't do without you... Good God,' she moaned, catching a glimpse of herself in the mirror, 'is that me?'

She touched the skin under her eyes, running her fingers lightly along the dark circles. Her hair was stiff with the remnants of the spray that kept it in place during the long hours at the Rooster. The shapeless pants and sweater were the final touch.

'Would you let this person take care of your child?' she asked her reflection.

The answer, of course, was 'no'. You wouldn't let this woman walk your dog. There was an old-fashioned sterling silver hairbrush on the dresser, heavily inlaid with mother-of-pearl. She snatched it up and brushed it through her hair. Better, she thought, but not by much. Appearances counted in this world—all you had to do was ask any of the waitresses at the Rooster whether

their tips didn't go up as their necklines went down—
and so far David Griffin had seen her dressed for the
Golden Rooster and in this scruffy outfit that made her
look like a homeless derelict. Neither image inspired
confidence, and she was sure image was what counted
with someone like him.

The car had told her that, and the house confirmed
it. Each room that she'd seen—and she hadn't seen them
all—was furnished for maximum effect. None of them
felt lived in, except for that terrible one with the hawk
and the musty tapestries, and no sane person would call
that 'lived in'. The house was a beautiful façade, designed, no doubt, to tell the world that David Griffin
was a man of wealth and power. His clothes were like
that, too. She'd have bet his closets were filled with rows
of custom-made three-piece suits, each the same except
for colour. Yesterday, he had substituted a navy pinstripe for the grey pinstripe before he left for the city.

'There's a problem at my office,' he had said just after
they'd sat down to breakfast. 'I may be late. I probably
won't see you until tomorrow.'

And that was the last she'd seen of him, thank
goodness. If her luck held, maybe he'd be gone for the
day. Maybe...

A peal of laughter rose from outside the french doors.
It was an infectious sound, especially in a place as
humourless as this. The house was like a museum; you
had the feeling people whispered all the time. The
laughter came again, and Rachel's lips twitched in an
answering smile. She put down the comb and crossed
the room, pulling the doors open and stepping out on
the balcony.

The lawn behind the house, as yet untouched by
autumn frost, was a green carpet that extended to the
river glistening like a silver ribbon far in the distance.
Immediately below the balcony, the gardener had raked

together a pile of dry leaves, and in the centre of that pile, Jamie sat astride a man whose face she could not see. All that were visible to her were his long, dungaree-clad legs and dusty boots. The laughter she had heard was the child's and the man's, mingling together as he bounced the baby on his knees. Jamie was hanging on to the man's hands, although every now and then he pulled one chubby hand free, seized a handful of leaves and flung them into the man's face. Rachel's smile broadened. Turning the baby over to the gardener for a morning's romp was a strange way for Emma to care for her charge, and it was a factor Rachel would use to her advantage when she made a case for letting her be responsible for Jamie, but she had to admit the man and the boy were having a good time.

She turned back towards the doors just as the child squealed with joy. Automatically, she looked down again, her lips curving upward in a smile. She'd have to introduce herself to the gardener and thank the man for...

No, she thought, the smile freezing on her mouth. The man was getting to his feet, swinging Jamie into the air and on to his shoulder—and it was David, not the gardener, David, dressed in clothes scruffier than hers, his face alive with laughter and happiness. A cold fist clamped around her heart as she watched him draw the child's head down to his. Jamie planted a kiss on David's cheek and then his fat little arms wrapped around his neck.

She slammed the french doors behind her and leaned against them. Panic engulfed her and turned to anger.

'How dare he?' she said aloud, her voice trembling. 'How dare he come from out of nowhere and think he can take over?'

She yanked open the bedroom door and stormed down the stairs, hurrying past an astonished maid in the foyer.

Emma looked up in surprise as she strode into the kitchen.

'Good morning, Miss Cooper. Would you like...'

Rachel ignored her and hurried out of the back door. There was another way out to the rear lawn—there were probably ten other ways, she thought grimly—but you needed a map to find them and she was in too much of a hurry to wander from room to room searching for exits. David Griffin couldn't just shove her aside. She wouldn't permit it...

'Miss? Is something wrong?'

The housekeeper's cry floated after her, a faint counterpoint to the dry leaves crunching loudly beneath her feet. Jamie smiled when he saw her but she ignored him, directing all her attention to David Griffin instead.

'Just what do you think you're doing?' she demanded.

David looked at her and one dark eyebrow rose. 'Is that really a question you need answered, Rachel? I think it's fairly obvious.'

'Yes,' she said grimly, 'it certainly is. How dare you?'

'I seem to have missed something here. How dare I what? Wake you so early in the day? I apologise for that, Rachel. I should have realised...'

'You know that's not what I meant,' she snapped. 'You were playing with Jamie—laughing with him...'

'Mr Griffin? Is everything all right?'

David nodded at the housekeeper who had come up behind Rachel. 'Yes, fine, Emma. Take the boy inside, will you?' He smiled as he handed the child to her. 'I think it's time for a nappy change. Now,' he added, his smile fading as he turned to Rachel, 'what is it I'm being accused of?'

'I know what you're doing, Mr Griffin.'

'Perhaps you'll let me in on it, Rachel.'

Her hands itched with the desire to slap the mocking smile from his face. 'You're trying to buy Jamie's love,' she said. 'But it won't work.'

His eyebrows rose again. 'Buy his love?'

Rachel nodded. 'All those toys in his bedroom . . . that crib that must have cost ten times what his old one did . . . and now this—this display this morning . . .'

'What display?' he asked mildly.

'You know what display!' she snapped furiously. 'Playing with him, laughing with him . . .'

Something was wrong with the way that sounded, she thought, and her words broke off suddenly. David Griffin nodded his head as he brushed bits of leaf from his wool shirt.

'Don't stop now,' he said. 'It was just getting interesting. I never thought of it that way before, Rachel. Are you suggesting it would be better for Jamie if I hadn't given him any toys? Well, it's a thought,' he mused, his voice thoughtful and serious. 'No toys, and what to sleep in? A box, perhaps, or a basket—although he's a bit large for a basket. Of course, I could have picked something up at the Salvation Army . . .'

How had he managed to turn her hurt into something laughable? Rachel shook her head and held up her hand.

'You know I didn't mean it that way . . .'

'And you're right about playing with him. What a hell of a thing to do with my own son. And laughing— God! Maybe you'd better report me to the authorities, after all.'

'I'm glad you find all this amusing,' she said angrily, 'but I don't see anything funny about it. You said I'd be taking care of Jamie. You said you understood that he needed me. You said you wanted me to help him adjust to all this . . .'

Suddenly the amused smile was gone. 'The truth, at last! You're afraid I've changed my mind. Is that it?'

You bastard, she thought. She took a deep breath and then another, swallowing her anger. 'No,' she lied, 'that's not it. I have to assume you're too astute a businessman to make an investment for no good reason.'

His eyebrows rose. 'Meaning what?'

She shrugged her shoulders, trying to keep her voice casual, afraid to let him see the depth of her fear.

'Meaning you know I can help you, even if you and Jamie are getting along well. He's at a difficult age—he can't make himself understood clearly yet. He says lots of things only I understand and it would take Emma quite a while to know what he means. And he prefers certain toys and foods...'

'Don't beg, Rachel,' said David. 'It doesn't become you. It isn't necessary. I've already agreed to let you stay. And I always keep my word. I told you that.'

She wanted to throw her arms in the air with joy, but she managed a polite smile. 'And if you'd let me spend more time with him... put him back into my room, for instance...'

His eyes turned to stones. 'Don't push,' he said softly.

So much for feeling victorious, she thought. 'But he needs me...'

'There's nothing further to discuss,' he said, turning away from her.

'There is,' she insisted. 'There are things you don't understand...' Her voice rose as he stalked away from her, his long strides carrying him quickly across the lawn. Rachel had to half run to keep up with him. 'Can't you wait a minute?' she gasped.

'I have work to do,' he said curtly.

Work, she thought, looking from the tips of his scuffed leather boots to his wool shirt, faded and soft with age—work? David Griffin was the kind of financial genius who made his own rules on Wall Street, but she doubted that even he showed up in those granite canyons dressed like this. They had reached a small building made of the same grey stone as the house. David pulled open the door and stepped aside. A garage? Yes, of course. He liked cars, or at least that was how it had sounded yesterday when he'd said something to the butler or the chauffeur or whoever in God's name Barton was...

She grabbed at the door as it began to swing shut. 'Let me talk to you while you do whatever it is you're going to... It's dark in here,' she said, uncertainty creeping into her voice. 'Can't you turn on a lamp or something?'

'Your eyes will get accustomed to the light in a few minutes,' he said, moving past her towards the centre of the room.

'This isn't a garage,' she said slowly.

David's laughter was sharp. 'No, it certainly isn't.'

'Is it a tool shed? A gardening shed?' Rachel's nose wrinkled and she stepped backwards. 'That smell,' she whispered. 'It's like yesterday...' Her eyes widened in the grey half-light of the room as they focused on something near David. 'The goshawk...'

The bird was sitting on a wooden perch, its great yellow eyes trained on her. Rachel took another step back as her glance raced around the room. There were other perches in the room, most of them empty, but there were two other birds near Isis, both smaller than she, both wearing elaborate leather helmets that somehow made them look even more deadly than the larger goshawk. Isis lifted herself and stretched her wings and tail outward. It made her look twice as large and a hundred times as frightening. Heart racing, Rachel took another stumbling step backwards.

'Stand still,' ordered David, and suddenly he was beside her, his hands biting into her shoulders. 'Just don't move. Isis is remembering yesterday. She's trying to impress you.'

'I'm impressed,' Rachel murmured. 'Can't she tell?'

'Give her a chance to see that you're not a threat. And give the other birds a chance to get used to you.'

'Give them a... Shouldn't that be the other way around?' she whispered. 'I'm the one who needs to get used to them. Anyway, they have hoods on. They can't see me...'

'They can hear you, Rachel. And believe me, they can sense fear.' His fingers spread on her shoulders, kneading her flesh. 'Just breathe normally—that's it. Now move forward a bit—come on. Nothing is going to happen.'

She ran her tongue over dry lips. 'What...what is this place?'

'It's a mews,' he said softly. 'It's where I keep my hawks.' A tremor ran through her, and she drew back until she was leaning against him. Some part of her brain registered the fact that she was pressed against David's body, that she could feel the hard, muscled planes of his chest and thighs against her, but all that seemed important was the comfort her trembling body took from the strength of his. 'There's nothing to be afraid of,' he murmured, his breath fanning her hair. 'The birds are more afraid of you than you could ever be of them.'

Nervous laughter bubbled in her throat. 'Don't I wish!' she said drily. 'Look, I'll wait outside.'

'I thought you wanted to talk to me.'

'I do, yes, but...'

'You'd better get used to the mews, Rachel. I spend a lot of time here, and Jamie will too.'

'Jamie? But he's just a baby!'

David laughed softly. 'He's my son,' he said. 'He'll learn to love these hawks as I do.'

Rachel shook her head. 'Not Jamie,' she said positively. 'He couldn't love these...these things. What are you doing?' she hissed as he urged her forward. 'Mr

Griffin...' She dug her feet into the earth floor. 'I'm not going another step!'

'Yes, you will, Rachel,' he said in a low whisper, then he laughed softly. 'And considering how close we've just become, don't you think it's time you stopped calling me Mr Griffin?'

She closed her eyes at the insinuating sound of his laughter and the heated pressure of his body against hers. Quickly she moved forward, letting his hands on her shoulders guide her towards the first perch.

'That's it,' he said softly. 'Another few inches...' His grip tightened, the pressure of his hands strangely comforting. 'There's nothing to fear, Rachel. Have you ever watched a hawk or a falcon soaring against the clouds, catching a thermal beneath its wings and sailing overhead?' His voice was soft, almost hypnotic. She nodded and he bent his head towards hers until his breath was warm against her ear. 'Have you ever wondered how the world must look from five hundred feet up? They're beautiful creatures, Rachel. And to gain the trust of one of them is very special. Come,' he said quietly, urging her forward again, 'let me introduce you.'

'It's OK, I...'

'This is Horus,' David said quietly, pausing before a grey bird slightly larger than a crow. 'He's a tercel—a male goshawk.'

'A goshawk? Like Isis? But he's smaller...'

David nodded. 'Yes, he is. Male hawks always are. Horus has had a hard life. He was taken from his nest by a kid out hunting birds' eggs. By the time I got him, he was half starved. The kid had been trying to feed him worms and beetles.' He reached out and stroked the tercel's breast. 'It was touch and go there for a while, wasn't it, boy?' The tercel cocked his head to one side at the touch and David smiled. 'Horus and I have made real progress.' His hands pressed into her shoulders and Rachel moved forward again.

'This is a hawk?' she asked softly, pausing before the next perch. 'It's even smaller than the other.'

David chuckled softly. 'But tough as nails. This is a kestrel. He flew into a window during migration and hurt his wing. He'll never be much of a flyer again, but he still enjoys getting up in the air on a good day, don't you, Fred?'

Nervous laughter bubbled in her throat again. 'Fred?' she repeated in disbelief. 'Fred the Hawk?'

David grinned. 'Terrible, isn't it? But kestrels are pretty common in these parts, and the game warden who found him had a weird sense of humour. He dubbed this little guy "Fred" and I'm afraid the name stuck.'

The kestrel was barely larger than a blue jay. Rachel stepped closer, watching the rapid rise and fall of its chest. The bird seemed to know she was there; its head, inside the leather hood, cocked to one side as she approached.

'Why are they hooded?' she whispered.

'They aren't always. Not being able to see calms them. They were a little upset this morning—the gardener was cleaning out the mews—and I hooded these two guys to get them to relax.' He reached past her and stroked the kestrel's breast. 'Would you like to see him?'

Rachel nodded. Slowly David opened the leather laces that kept the hood closed and drew it from the bird's head. The kestrel shook itself and stretched its wings. Rachel gasped and stumbled back.

'Easy,' said David, slipping his arm around her waist. 'He's just getting comfortable.' His fingers splayed across her hip, urging her forward again. 'Would you like to meet him?' She nodded again. 'Say hello to the lady, Fred,' he said softly. 'Touch him lightly with your finger, Rachel.'

She swallowed and then extended her index finger towards the kestrel. Hesitantly she ran the tip of her finger along the bird's breast.

'He's beautiful,' she whispered. 'And he's so warm— I knew he'd be soft, but I didn't expect him to be hot...'

'Their temperatures are much higher than ours,' David said quietly. 'He likes you, Rachel.'

'How can you tell?'

'See how he's fluffing his feathers out? That's called rousing. It means he's content.'

A smile flickered across her face. 'I've never touched a wild creature before,' she said softly.

David's fingers tightened on her waist. 'You have a gentle touch, Rachel. That can tame any wild heart.'

Suddenly she was aware of his closeness. She could feel the length of his body pressing against her back, feel the taut leanness of him against her thighs. Her head was against his chest; there was a soft thudding beneath her ear that she recognised as his heartbeat. A tingling sensation raced upwards from her fingertips. Was this the David Griffin Cassie had fallen for, the David Griffin who could charm any woman he wanted? The heat of his body seemed to engulf her, coaxing an answering response from hers. She closed her eyes, stunned at the way her senses were betraying her. Say something, she thought desperately, do something...

'Did Cassie like your hawks?' she asked.

She heard the intake of his breath. 'Cassie never met them,' he said. 'But then you'd know that, wouldn't you? You said you and she were very close—that she told you everything.'

Caught by your own glib tongue, Rachel thought. 'We were,' she said quickly, 'at least, we were when we were growing up. But during the last few years...she was busy,' she said, hating the defensive tone of her own voice. 'Modelling is a very demanding career. She had to devote all her time to it.'

'More demanding than your career? Didn't the Golden Rooster take a lot of your time too?'

His voice was silky with arrogant amusement. Rachel stiffened and tried to draw away from him, but his hands held her fast.

'Look, I'm tired of your insinuations, Mr Griffin...'

'David,' he said softly, pulling her more back against his body. 'Surely we're on a first-name basis now?'

She felt her face flood with colour. 'I put in eight hours a night, six days a week, at the Rooster. I was a waitress, that's all. It's... it was hardly a career.'

'Then why such dedication, Rachel?'

'Because it was a way to make good money,' she said, her voice rough with irritation.

'Ah, yes, I can imagine. The tips must have been excellent.'

There was an edge to the simple words that filled her with rage. She pulled free of his restraining hands and turned to face him.

'I was a waitress,' she said harshly. 'Nothing more. I used to be a secretary in an insurance company, but then Cassie died. I needed money for Jamie. And I needed to be with him during the day. I couldn't afford to pay for someone to care for him. That's when I became a cocktail waitress. Have we got that all straightened out now?'

She raised her chin defiantly and stared upwards into his face. His eyes met hers, the strange golden colour somehow softer than she remembered. His hands slid to her arms and he stepped backwards, holding her out before him as if she were an object to inspect, his glance travelling slowly from her face down her body. Finally he shook his head.

'You aren't much like Cassie at all, are you?'

Some things never changed, Rachel thought. She had lived with that kind of comment most of her life. It was years since it had hurt to be compared to Cassie—but a sudden pain knifed through her, although why this man's opinion should mean anything, one way or the other...

She squared her shoulders and shook her head. 'No, not in the least. She was always beautiful.'

'We'll have to see about having the rest of your clothes brought from your apartment,' he said. 'You do own something besides that sweater and those pants, don't you?'

Damn the man! she thought. It was bad enough that he'd reminded her of how much prettier Cassie had always been. Now he was making her feel not just plain but homely. Anger made her reckless.

'Of course,' she said evenly. 'I have my costume from the Golden Rooster.'

A sensual smile lifted the corners of his mouth. 'Yes,' he murmured, 'I remember.' His glance flickered across her again. 'I remember very well.'

Rachel swallowed drily. 'Mr Griffin...'

'David,' he corrected.

'Mr Griffin, I...'

He shook his head. 'David,' he repeated, in that voice she knew so well, a voice that was accustomed to giving orders. 'We don't want to confuse Jamie, do we? The servants call me Mr Griffin, Rachel. Jamie has to learn the difference.'

There was something wrong with his logic, she thought, but it was impossible to argue with him. He was too overpowering, too used to being obeyed. And he was too close to her, his hands holding her too tightly...

'David,' she said at last, 'I think we should talk about Jamie. He...'

'You really love the boy, don't you?'

She looked at him in amazement. 'Yes, of course I do. Why wouldn't I?'

'What did Cassie tell you about me, Rachel?'

'I told you—everything.'

His eyes locked with hers. 'Everything,' he repeated, and she nodded. 'Are you sure?'

'Of course I'm sure. She always told me...' A knowing smile flickered across his face and Rachel tossed her head. 'All right, not always. But she told me all about...about you, and how you...you...'

'How I seduced her?' he prompted, his voice soft and insinuating. Rachel nodded again and he smiled. 'And how did I do that? Did she tell you all the details?'

A swift rush of heat washed over her. 'Yes,' she said abruptly, then shook her head. 'Well, no, of course not the details.'

'Cassie lied to you,' he said roughly.

'No—she wouldn't. She...'

His fingers were kneading her shoulders. She wanted to move away from him, from the dark shadows in the mews, but all the strength seemed to have left her.

'Yes,' he murmured, 'she lied. Maybe she lied about everything.'

Hope surged within her breast. 'About Jamie, you mean?'

He shook his head. 'Jamie's mine—you know that.'

Rachel wanted to deny it, but she couldn't, not after seeing those two dark heads together, not after seeing the baby's face reflected in the man's. She drew a breath and shook her head.

'I don't understand,' she whispered. 'I don't...'

'Yes, you do,' he said hoarsely, 'you understand this.'

And then his mouth slanted down hungrily across hers, warm and hard. His hands slid to her waist, his fingers curving around her hips, bringing her tightly against him. For a heart-stopping second she fought against him, against the intrusion of his lips on hers, against his tongue forcing her lips apart, and then a glow seemed to infuse her and her mouth opened to his. His arms drew her closer as his mouth moved hungrily over hers. Suddenly there was a shrill, piercing cry from across the room. The hair rose on the back of Rachel's neck and she pushed free of David's arms.

'What was that?' she whispered.

He laughed softly. 'That was Isis. I think she was telling us she doesn't like what we were doing.'

Rachel breathed a silent prayer of thanks. 'She's a smart bird,' she said in a voice that amazed her with its steadiness. 'Neither did I.'

She brushed past him and flung the door open. As she hurried out into the bright sunlight, she wondered whether her lie had sounded more convincing to him than it had to her.

CHAPTER FOUR

'SUCH a lovely day, miss... There won't be many more before winter.'

Startled, Rachel looked up from her book. The housekeeper's friendly face smiled at her from the open nursery doorway.

'Emma, I...I didn't hear you come in. I was sitting here while Jamie napped.'

Damn! she thought angrily. She hadn't meant to sound like a child caught with her hand in the cookie jar.

'Barton just brought in some apples,' the housekeeper told her, putting a bowl of shining red fruit on the dressing table. 'From our own orchard. Aren't they lovely? Won't you try one?'

'No, thank you, I...' The woman's homely face was filled with mute appeal. After a moment Rachel nodded and took an apple from the bowl. 'Thank you, Emma. It's very thoughtful of you.'

'You don't eat enough to keep a bird alive, Miss Cooper. It's not healthy.'

'I don't have much appetite lately. I guess I'm just not used to having so little to do.' Rachel glanced at her watch and closed her book. 'I'll go check on Jamie. He's probably...'

'I just looked, miss. The boy's sound asleep.' Emma looked at Rachel and her expression softened. 'You can check for yourself, if you like.'

Rachel shook her head. 'No, that's all right, Emma. I...' Suddenly the house seemed stifling. 'Maybe I'll go for a walk. You're right—it's a beautiful day.'

61

'Good idea, Miss Cooper. I'll be here to care for the baby when he awakens.'

There was nothing new in that, Rachel thought as she shrugged into her jacket. Only a few days had passed, but she could feel Jamie slipping away from her. She looked at the apple she held in her hands and sighed. Emma meant well, she thought, dropping the apple into her pocket. If the woman found Rachel's presence a mystery, she hid it carefully. And she tried to let Rachel spend time with the child, but it was Emma who dressed him in the mornings, Emma who took him downstairs, Emma who fed him breakfast and lunch and never questioned Rachel's constant presence. And it was Emma who had seen to it that Jamie was all Rachel's in the evenings.

'I can't get the boy to sleep, sir,' she had told David the first night, a worried expression on her plump features. 'He keeps asking for... for his mother.'

The look David had given Rachel had turned her blood to ice. Then, after a moment, he'd nodded.

'Very well, Emma. Miss Cooper will attend to the child this evening.'

That one evening had stretched into three. David left the house early in the mornings and returned after dark, which meant he wasn't there to change what had become a nightly routine, and Emma seemed willing to let the arrangement stand. There were times Rachel wondered if he'd forgotten she was there. He'd certainly forgotten about having her clothing packed and sent to her, she thought, glancing down at her shiny corduroys as she opened the front door. Jamie's things had arrived, along with endless boxes of expensive clothing for the child, but not hers. Was David waiting for her to ask? Yes, she thought grimly, that would be just like him. She'd had to beg to stay with Jamie, beg to be allowed to spend time with him... Humiliating her seemed to be the man's pleasure, she thought, forcing back an unbidden image of what had happened in the mews. That was all that kiss had been.

David Griffin could rot in hell before she gave him another chance to make a fool of her! she thought grimly, striding across the grass. The trousers and sweater and lingerie that had been washed and re-washed during the past few days could dissolve into shreds first. There was such a thing as self-respect.

'Dammit, woman, watch where you're going!' The angry snarl of a deep voice cut her like a whip, and Rachel stumbled back as a horse, black as night, reared up in front of her. The animal whinnied in alarm and danced nervously under its rider. David Griffin stared down at her, his face a dark cloud.

'You're the one who should watch where he's going,' she said, as soon as she could get her voice under control. 'What were you trying to do, Mr Griffin? Run me down?'

'Is that the way you cross streets in New York?' he demanded. 'It's a wonder you get from one side to the other!'

She looked up at him with distaste. 'The wonder is that you haven't killed anybody yet,' she said, stuffing her shaking hands into her jacket pockets. 'I don't have any trouble crossing streets, Mr Griffin. I don't have any trouble crossing bridle paths in Central Park, either. They have signs posted to warn people that they're liable to be trampled to death.'

David's scowl vanished and his teeth flashed whitely. 'Trampling people isn't Abdullah's style,' he said, leaning over the horse's arched neck and patting the glistening black coat. The animal snorted nervously. 'Easy, boy,' he murmured. 'It's OK.' His eyes met Rachel's and the scowl reappeared. 'You scared the hell out of my horse.'

Rachel tossed the hair back from her face and laughed sharply. 'My God,' she said, sarcasm underscoring every word, 'I'd hate to think I'd done that. Maybe I should send him a note of apology.'

'A pat on the nose would do. He's really very easy to please.'

She gave the horse a sideways glance and shook her head. 'I make it a habit not to apologise to things that try to kill me. Let Abdullah talk things over with your hawk—they'll have lots to tell each other. Good day, Mr Griffin.'

Turning on her heel, she started back towards the house at a brisk pace, ignoring the muffled sounds of hoofbeats on the grass behind her. But she couldn't ignore the sudden not so gentle shove in the small of her back.

'Call your horse off, please,' she said evenly, trying to keep her footing as the finely chiselled head nuzzled her again.

David chuckled softly as the horse butted her once more. 'Its his idea, not mine. He likes you, Rachel.'

She glanced quickly behind her. The horse was following her, it's head almost at her shoulder.

'I'm delighted to hear it,' she said, quickening her pace. 'Tell him the feeling's not... Hey!' she protested indignantly, as the animal pushed its nose into her back. 'Look, Mr Griffin...'

'David. I thought we settled that the other day.'

His voice was silken and the message subtle. Rachel felt her cheeks blaze, but at least her back was to him. It couldn't be much fun humiliating her if he couldn't see her face.

'I'm sorry I disturbed you and whatever his name is...'

'Abdullah. And you didn't disturb us, Rachel. Abdullah and I...' His words dissolved in laughter as the horse tried to bury his nose in Rachel's pocket.

'He's going to rip my jacket,' she said angrily, stopping and turning to face the horse. 'Tell him...'

'Tell him yourself. You've been holding out. No wonder he's willing to follow you anywhere!'

'Holding out?' she repeated, while the horse nuzzled his way into her pocket. 'I don't know what you're talking about. I...' The stream of indignant words slowed as Abdullah lifted his head in triumph, the apple Emma had pressed upon her in his teeth. 'I didn't know that was there,' Rachel said lamely. 'Well, I knew, but...' She watched as the horse crunched down on the fruit with amazing delicacy, his dark eyes rolling with pleasure. Despite herself, she began to smile. 'You're a thief, Abdullah,' she said softly. 'That was supposed to be my dessert.'

David chuckled as he swung down from the saddle. 'He's a sucker for apples and sugar,' he said, running his hand along the animal's withers. 'You won't regret this, Rachel. He'll be your friend for life.'

She smiled as the horse swallowed the fruit and moved towards her again. 'No more,' she said, letting the velvety nose investigate her pocket. 'See? It's empty.'

'He'll want to check the other one... OK, now he'll let you alone. I'm afraid he's ripped your pocket,' he said, running his finger along the fabric. 'Here, at the seam.'

His touch on her jacket was light, but she felt as if his hand was on her naked skin, searing her flesh through the layers of clothing. Nervousness sharpened her voice.

'Then I'll just have to fix it,' she said, starting across the grass. 'Especially since it's the only jacket I have.'

'The only...' She felt David's eyes on her, travelling the length of her body from her scuffed sneakers to her ripped jacket, and then he burst out laughing.

Dammit, she thought furiously, she'd set herself up for that. Hadn't she promised herself she wouldn't say anything about her clothing? And now she'd made that stupid comment...

'It isn't funny,' she said with dignity. 'I need my things.'

His hand caught hers and he tugged her around until she faced him. 'Rachel, I'm so sorry. Are you saying you've had nothing to wear except that one outfit?'

'Are you saying you didn't know that?' she demanded.

David ran his hand through his hair. 'Of course I didn't. I got involved in a takeover that almost fell apart and... Hell, why didn't you say something?' She shrugged. 'Dammit, Rachel, you could have told Emma, if you were so intent on avoiding me!'

'I was not intent on avoiding you, Mr Griffin. I...'

'David,' he corrected.

'I've been managing,' she answered, avoiding the use of his name. 'Emma showed me where the laundry-room is.'

'What kind of man do you think I am, Rachel?' He shook his head and stepped back, his eyes going over her again, lingering on the rapid rise and fall of her breasts beneath the open jacket. 'You're one surprise after another,' he said softly. 'Somehow I can't picture Cassie wearing the same scruffy outfit day after day.'

'You're right,' she said quickly, trying unsuccessfully to free her hand from his. 'Cassie probably would have managed to look stunning even in rags. I told you we were very different. I...'

'Cassie wouldn't have kept quiet all this time. She'd have registered her protests in no uncertain terms.' David moved a step closer, his eyes locked with hers. 'Don't you care about things like that, Rachel?'

Embarrassment licked hotly at her. What did it matter what he thought of her looks? she told herself, but her cheeks felt as if they were blazing just the same.

'I told you, I've been washing these things. I may not be a fashion plate, but I'm clean, and that's all that counts. Jamie...'

David smiled and let go of Abdullah's reins. 'I wasn't thinking of Jamie,' he said softly, laying his hand along her cheek. 'I was thinking of me.'

'You don't have to worry about me disgracing your house. I keep to my room. No one sees me.'

Suddenly his voice was a scourge. 'Lots of people saw you at the Golden Rooster.' His hand slipped down her jaw and cupped her chin, his fingers pressing into her flesh. 'How did it feel to have all those men staring at you, Rachel? Didn't it bother you to know what they were thinking?'

Anger sharpened her tongue. 'And you'd know what they were thinking, wouldn't you? You were there for hours, Mr Griffin, and your eyes never left me!'

She held her breath, watching as his face darkened and his eyes burned their golden heat into hers. She forced herself not to flinch from their blazing ferocity. Finally, to her surprise, an unwilling smile touched the corners of his mouth.

'Maybe you're right,' he said softly.

'And aren't you disappointed to find out that this is the real me?' she asked, wrenching away from him. 'You can't judge a book by its cover. Just because you saw me at the Golden Rooster...'

'Industry spends a lot of time and money on fancy packaging, Rachel.'

'And it's all to get people to buy the product. The Rooster's product is overpriced booze. All it proves is that a fool and his money...'

A quick grin lit his face. '...are soon parted. Have you got a homespun proverb for every occasion?'

Her hands went to her hips. 'Does that strike you as amusing?'

The grin broadened, softening the harsh planes in his face. 'I've got to admit it's unusual to hear them coming from someone like you.'

'Someone like me? Are we back to the costume I wore at the Rooster?'

David sighed with resignation. 'Someone as young as you, is what I meant, Rachel.'

'I'm not a child!'

'Ah, forgive me. Yours is the voice of an older generation.'

He was laughing at her. She could hear it in his voice and see it the tiny lines at the corners of his eyes. Why hadn't she realised those were laugh lines? she wondered suddenly. Why had she assumed they were only lines he'd got from squinting at the sun?

'My grandmother used those sayings all the time. And they all make sense, when you think about it,' she said defensively.

'Oh, I agree,' he said softly. He took a step back and let his gaze drift slowly over her. 'I never said I was disappointed in the real you, Rachel. I like what I see. In fact, I like the real Rachel Cooper much more than I thought I would.'

Rachel's face flushed. 'That's easy to understand. You didn't expect to like her at all.'

He laughed softly. 'So tell me, Rachel Cooper, what have you done with yourself the past few days? Do you miss the city?'

The sudden change of subject took her by surprise. 'Of course I miss it,' she said immediately, then she shook her head. It seemed stupid to pretend to miss her cramped apartment and the narrow streets of her lower Manhattan neighbourhood, still hot and steaming in the late days of Indian summer. 'No,' she admitted, 'not particularly.'

David nodded. 'And your job? I take it you don't miss that.'

Rachel shoved her hands into her trouser pockets and started slowly across the lawn. David scooped up Abdullah's trailing reins and walked beside her.

'Look, Mr Griffin...'

'Come now, Rachel,' he said softly, 'we're on a first-name basis, remember? Do you need a reminder?'

'Look, David, if you're waiting for me to thank you for this...this vacation at summer camp, you've got a long wait ahead of you. My apartment was—is—a hole in the wall and my job's horrible, but that doesn't mean I'm pleased to be here.' She glanced up at him and took a breath. 'Everything had a purpose until you...until you decided you wanted Jamie. I hated the Golden Rooster, but it paid the bills. I worked hard, but the time went quickly. I...'

'Emma tells me you've kept yourself busy.'

'I haven't broken our agreement,' she said quickly. 'You said you wanted me to ease things for Jamie.'

'She says you helped her bake the other day.'

'I just wanted to feel useful. Did I violate some rule? I thought...'

David's mouth twisted. 'You really think I'm a bastard, don't you? No, you didn't violate any rule. The only thing I'm trying to do is make Jamie less dependent on you. Am I a monster because I want my son?'

'How simple you make it sound!'

'It is simple.'

'Why didn't you think of your son months ago?' she asked bitterly.

David grasped her wrist and swung her towards him. 'Dammit, woman, you can't have it both ways! You hate me for wanting him and you hate me for *not* wanting him. Which is it?'

'Maybe if you'd wanted him from the start...'

His eyes narrowed dangerously. 'Are we back to that again?'

'We never left it. When Cassie was pregnant...'

'How in God's name was I supposed to know it was my child she was carrying?' he demanded angrily. 'Every man in New York...'

'Don't!' she said in a warning whisper.

'There's no use in trying to deny it. There were a dozen men before me and a dozen...'

All the anger Rachel had so carefully controlled during the past few days ignited. 'Liar!' she breathed, her hand a blur as it struck his cheek. 'Cassie wasn't like that.'

He touched his fingers to his cheek, where the red imprint of her hand lay. 'Yes,' he said softly, his eyes seeking hers, 'yes, she was. You must have known. Everyone else did. I can understand that you loved her, but that doesn't change the truth. You can't go on lying to yourself for ever.'

'I'm not! I...I...' His eyes sought hers, catching and holding them until finally she bowed her head. 'It's pointless to argue over this. She's gone. All that matters is now.'

His breath hissed sharply. 'I agree.'

'Do you have any idea of how much Jamie means to me?'

His hand fell from her wrist. 'You keep asking me that, Rachel, as if you were the only person involved in this.'

'I'm not forgetting you're his...his father,' she said quickly. 'But I love him. I...'

'Then stop being so damned selfish. Would you want him to grow up without his father?'

Her eyes closed and she sighed. 'No,' she admitted, her voice a husky whisper. 'But why did you wait so long? All this would have made sense if you'd come months ago.'

'All right,' David said harshly. His hand closed around her wrist again. 'I have to take Abdullah back to the stables. Walk with me, Rachel. Maybe you're right. Maybe you're entitled to know more.'

She glanced at him, surprise reflected in her eyes, but she said nothing, matching her stride to his as they walked slowly towards the stone outbuildings that housed the stables. He said nothing for a long while, and she thought he had reconsidered, until finally he took a deep breath.

'I didn't believe Cassie when she told me she was pregnant with my child,' he said slowly. 'But you already know that.'

'Yes, but you should have. She wouldn't have lied, not about something like that. I knew her almost all her life. She...'

'I'm not going to argue with you, Rachel,' he said flatly. 'We're all entitled to our memories. Besides, all that's important is the present. You said so yourself.' She sighed and nodded her head, and his hand tightened on her wrist. 'When I heard Cassie had over... when I heard she'd died, I began to think about the child.'

'My grandmother would have loved you,' Rachel said stiffly. 'Better late than never, right?'

'Dammit, Rachel, do you want to hear this or don't you?'

She sighed with resignation. 'Go on.'

'I didn't always have this place, you know.' His voice dropped to a whisper; she had to step closer to him in order to hear what he was saying. 'I got what I have on my own.'

There was a curious flatness to the statement, a lack of whatever inflection would have made the comment sound like a prideful boast. Rachel waited for him to say more, but his cryptic comment was evidently all the explanation he was going to make.

'Look,' she said quietly, 'I know you want to share things with Jamie. I don't blame you for wanting an heir.'

His fingers bit into her flesh and she winced with pain. 'Is that what you think this is all about? Wanting an heir?' Gradually his grip lessened and he laughed. The sound was soft and bitter. 'I want to give the boy a father, Rachel. What I'm trying to tell you is that I know what it's like to be raised without one. I spent my childhood in an orphanage.'

The words sounded strangely devoid of emotion, delivered in the same flat tone he had used to describe how he had acquired his holdings. Surprised, Rachel stopped and turned to face him. His eyes were dark with memories, and the corners of his mouth were pulled downward. Automatically she reached out to him, stopping herself only at the last second.

'I'm so sorry, David.'

For the first time, his name came easily to her lips, but he shrugged aside her sympathy.

'This isn't an appeal for pity,' he said harshly.

'I didn't think it was. All I meant was, I didn't know.'

'Nobody knows,' he said. 'It's not anybody's damned business except my own. I'm only telling you so you understand...' He took a deep breath and ran his hand through his hair in a gesture that was becoming familiar to her. 'Look, all I'm trying to say is that the boy needs me now. When I planned all this—well, I didn't know you. I thought...I thought you were going to be like...' Her eyes darkened and David held up his hand. 'Let's not argue about her, Rachel. All I'm trying to say is that I'm sorry I've hurt you in the process.'

She felt a quick surge of hope. 'Do you mean that, David?' He nodded his head and she took a breath. 'Then we can find some sort of compromise, can't we? I don't have to be locked out of Jamie's life.' She reached out to him again and put her hand on his arm. 'We can find a way, I know we can.'

'There you are, David! I've been looking everywhere.' The sound of the strange female voice fell between them like cold rain. David looked up in surprise.

'Vanessa——What are you doing here?'

Rachel looked at the tall, elegant figure walking towards them. Unconsciously her hand went to her hair and then to her jacket pocket, trying to hide the rip in it. The woman smiled benignly.

'You must be Rachel,' she said.

'Yes. I...'

Her smile broadened. 'How do you do, Rachel? I'm Miss Walters.'

The reminder of her status as a servant was subtle but purposeful. Rachel's hand fell from David's arm and she took a step back.

'Jamie must be awake by now,' she murmured. 'I'll head back to the house.'

'Rachel...'

The woman ran her hand familiarly along Abdullah's flank and then laced her arm through David's. 'Let her go, David. You can show her around the property some other time. If we don't hurry, you'll never be ready by six o'clock. And you know you promised me you'd be on time.'

The slender body lounged carelessly against his. For no reason she could determine, Rachel felt a coldness race through her.

'It's almost time for Jamie's bath,' she said, turning away from the scene before her. 'I have to go.'

'We haven't finished talking, Rachel. I...'

She whirled towards David, fighting against the sudden desire to strike him again.

'I won't do anything I haven't your permission to do,' she said coldly. 'You don't have to worry.'

'Rachel, wait . . .'

'David, please—let the woman do her job.' Vanessa Walters smiled slowly and leaned her head towards his while her voice dropped to a conspiratorial whisper. 'Let's put Abdullah in and then go to your rooms. You can shower while I lay out your things. The blue suit tonight, don't you think? You look so distinguished in that.'

She tilted her face up to David's. Behind them, Abdullah raised his head. A dry leaf, red as blood, clung to his velvet muzzle. Inexplicably, tears stung Rachel's eyes and she turned away quickly and hurried back to the safety of the house. Her room was no longer a prison but a haven.

CHAPTER FIVE

'EMMA? Emma!' Rachel's voice was breathless with indignation as she pushed open the kitchen door.

The housekeeper looked up from a pile of carrot peelings that lay on the chopping block. 'Is something wrong, miss?' she asked mildly.

'Yes, something's wrong. I just put Jamie to bed, and when I went back to my room, there was a stack of boxes on the bed.'

The woman arched her eyebrows and nodded. 'Ah, yes. They were delivered earlier this afternoon, while you and Jamie were in the garden. They're from Lord & Taylor.'

'I know where they're from,' Rachel said sharply. 'I can read the labels. Did Mr Griffin send them, Emma?'

The housekeeper shrugged. 'I should think so, miss.'

Rachel nodded grimly. 'Yes, well, he can send them right back. I told Barton to tell Mr Griffin that I wasn't... Please call the store and have them picked up.'

Emma looked down at her hands. 'I'm afraid I can't do that.'

'I'll call, then. I...'

'You can try, miss, but I think they'll want to hear from Mr Griffin first.'

Rachel's eyes narrowed. 'Yes,' she said sharply. 'I suppose they would.'

'May I help you with something else, miss?'

Rachel shook her head. There was no more sense in arguing with Emma than there had been in arguing with Barton earlier that morning, she thought as she stalked back up the stairs to her room. The butler had knocked on her door just past eight a.m.

'Who is it?' she'd asked, glancing at her watch in surprise. Jamie was already in the kitchen with Emma. She had heard the housekeeper in the boy's room almost an hour before.

'Barton,' he had said. 'I have a message for you, Miss Cooper.'

Rachel had opened the door an inch or so. 'Good morning, Barton,' she had said, peering out at him from behind the protective cover of the door. 'What's the message?'

'Good morning, miss,' he said politely. 'Mr Griffin said to ask if you wanted me to bring the car around now or wait until later.'

Rachel's glance took in the man's impassive expression and then skimmed down his dark jacket to his sharply pressed trousers and highly polished shoes. Without thinking, she moved further behind the door, hoping he couldn't see her bare feet or her increasingly disreputable-looking trousers and sweater.

'The car?' she asked blankly. 'What do I want the car for?'

'To go shopping, miss. If you wish to go into Manhattan, we should leave fairly soon. Mr Griffin said I was to take you wherever you preferred, either into the city or somewhere local.'

It was early, Rachel thought fuzzily. Maybe that was why she didn't understand any of this. She smiled tentatively.

'Shopping for what, Barton? Did Mr Griffin say Jamie needed something?' The man shook his head and Rachel frowned. 'Did Emma?'

'I'm to take you shopping for clothes for yourself, Miss Cooper. Mr Griffin thought you might like the new

Lord & Taylor branch that opened in a shopping mall down the road.'

'I see.' Rachel's mouth narrowed with determination. 'Tell Mr Griffin I don't want to go to Lord & Taylor. Tell him...'

The man nodded. 'Yes, that was what Miss Walters thought. She said you'd prefer Sears.'

Rachel's eyes lifted to Barton's, but his expression was unreadable. 'Sears?' she asked softly. 'Did she really?' He nodded uncomfortably. 'Well, you can tell Mr Griffin and Miss Walters that they were both wrong,' Rachel said coldly. 'I have no desire to go to either store. I have no wish to buy any clothing. I have my own...' Barton's eyes flickered over her and she flushed. 'My things are in my apartment,' she said. 'In New York.' She caught her lip between her teeth. 'You did offer to drive me to New York, didn't you?' she asked with sudden eagerness. He nodded and she smiled happily. 'Well, that's fine. My apartment's in lower Manhattan. There are some things there I'd like to pick up.'

Barton shook his head. 'I'm sorry, miss, I can't do that. Mr Griffin only said I was to take you shopping. If you want to make a change in plans, you'll have to take it up with him.'

'But...'

'Sorry, miss.'

Rachel clamped her jaws and forced a smile. 'Don't worry about it,' she said through her teeth. 'Thank you anyway.'

She had managed to keep the smile on her face until the door had closed. Then she'd mouthed a short, harsh word that Grandma had once washed out of her mouth with soap and water.

A gilded prison, she thought, looking around the expensively furnished room. And David Griffin was the warder. Angrily, she'd pulled on her shabby sneakers, pulling the laces so tightly one tore in half. 'Damn,' she muttered, tying the ripped ends together. David couldn't keep her locked up like this. She'd go right downstairs and tell him so. His car was still in the driveway. He...

Rachel had paused with her hand on the doorknob. He'd only smile and tell her she was free to leave whenever she liked. All she had to do was walk away from Jamie. She sank down on the bed, head hanging in defeat. The house was a prison without walls.

She'd waited until David's car finally left the driveway. The temptation to peep and see whether he was alone or with Vanessa Walters was strong, but she'd fought against it. What did it matter to her if the woman had spent the night here or not? The Jaguar had roared out of the driveway while Rachel was eating dinner in her room the previous evening, and it had been almost dawn before she'd heard it return. Not that it mattered. Not that it was any of her business...

At least David was letting her spend more time with Jamie. Emma hadn't said a word when Rachel had scooped the boy from his highchair.

'Morning, sweetness,' she'd said to him, and he'd laughed with delight.

'Mama?'

The single word had wrenched at her heart. 'I'm taking him for a walk,' she had said defiantly, but Emma had only nodded.

'Fine,' she had said placidly. 'Mr Griffin said it would be all right.'

'Mr Griffin said it would be all right,' muttered Rachel now, eyeing the elegant boxes from one of the East Coast's most elegant stores with distaste. Mr Griffin said breathe and everybody breathed. Mr Griffin said jump and everybody jumped. God, the man was awful! Which reminded her... It was time to get her dinner from Emma and bring it to her room. It was almost six-thirty. He might be home soon.

Rachel got to her feet and started to the door, but halfway there, her sneaker caught on something and she stumbled. The sole of one sneaker had parted company with the rest of the shoe. She hopped back to the bed and sank down on it, staring at her foot. The rubber sole hung from the instep of the sneaker like a dog's tongue on a hot summer day. With a sigh, Rachel grabbed the sole and ripped it free.

'Terrific,' she murmured glumly. That puts the finishing touch to it, she thought, staring at herself in the mirror. Now she looked absolutely perfect. Her oversized sweater was shapeless, and her cords were so thin they were worn through in spots. Without willing it, her gaze travelled across the room to the Lord & Taylor boxes. Sears, the Walters woman had said, but David had known she'd prefer the quiet elegance of Lord & Taylor to the economical briskness of Sears.

What a strange man he was turning out to be! The Hawk was a dove when it came to some things. He was fierce, yes—but not with his horse or his hawks. Or with his son, Rachel admitted, remembering how easily he and Jamie played together. She could almost picture David as a child, alone, without family, desperate for someone who would care...

'He's your enemy, Rachel,' she said aloud, stalking towards the boxes. 'Don't ever forget that. Just wait until the next time you see him. You can tell him what he can do with these things.'

Of course, she could also swallow her pride and thank him for his thoughtfulness. *You can catch more flies with honey than with vinegar, Rachel.* Stop that, Grandma! she thought fiercely, but finally with a shrug of resignation, she bent and opened a box at random. A pale blue cashmere dress lay within folds of white tissue paper.

She lifted it in her hands, letting the soft fabric drape across her fingers. It was the right size, the right colour. It couldn't hurt to slip the dress on. Not for just a minute or two.

She was twirling barefoot before the mirror, her hair still wet from the shower, telling herself she was merely checking the dress's length, when there was a knock at the door. Rachel's expression sobered. She snatched up her old sweater, holding it before her like a shield.

'Yes?' she said, opening the door a fraction of an inch.

Emma smiled at her. 'Dinner, miss. Mr Griffin said to tell you it was ready.'

'Is he here tonight?' The woman nodded. 'I guess he doesn't know I eat in my room, Emma. Would you tell him for me, please?'

'He said to tell you to join him out on the terrace for drinks, first, miss.'

'Emma,' Rachel said patiently, 'I said...'

'The boy's asleep. You needn't worry about him. And I'd wear a sweater or a scarf, miss—it's a cool evening.'

'Emma, how do you manage to hear only what you want to? I said...'

The housekeeper's shoulders rose expressively. 'I heard you, Miss Cooper. I'm only doing as I was told.' The tip of the woman's tongue appeared between her lips and she leaned forward. 'He said I wasn't to serve you any more trays, miss,' she whispered. 'You'll have to take your meals downstairs.'

'Did he really?' Rachel's voice was ice. 'Thank you, Emma. We'll see about that.'

She slammed the door and leaned against it. The Lord of the Manor, she thought—that's who David Griffin thought he was. Just hold up the hoop and everybody jumps. Well, she thought grimly, not this time.

Her hands trembled with anger as she stripped off the cashmere dress and tossed it aside.

'The hell with honey, Grandma. I'd rather get my flies with a swatter,' she muttered, pulling her old sweater over her head. 'Only in this case, I wish I had a...a ball bat.' She snatched up her cords and began stepping into them. 'I wish...'

There was the sound of fabric tearing and Rachel looked down at herself in stunned disbelief. Her bare toes had ripped one leg of the old pants from thigh to ankle. Furiously she pulled the cords off and kicked them across the room along with her sweater. With a determined grimace, she snatched up the discarded cashmere dress and slipped it over her head, smoothing the soft folds of the skirt as it settled about her hips.

'In for a penny, in for a pound, right, Grandma?' she murmured, slipping her feet into black kidskin pumps. The heels were foolishly high—not the kind she'd teetered along on at the Rooster, of course—but the shoes fitted well. In fact, everything fitted well, from the dress to the shoes to the lace underthings and sheer stockings.

Moments later, Rachel let the terrace door slam shut behind her. 'Didn't you understand what I told Barton this morning?' she said without preamble. 'I have my own clothing. It's back at my apartment. All somebody has to do is take me there.'

David was standing at the edge of the terrace, watching the sun sink behind the mountains. He turned at the sound of her voice and smiled.

'And good evening to you too, Rachel. I see you decided to join me for dinner. How nice!'

'Don't play with me, Mr Griffin!'

'Is your memory always this poor, or is it my name that's hard to remember?'

'Don't play games with me, David. You issued orders about my joining you for dinner. And you issued orders about this...'

She tugged at the blue dress and he smiled. 'It looks lovely, Rachel. But I don't recall ordering you to wear it this evening. Although it's a good choice...'

'Stop that!' she snapped, stamping her foot against the stone floor. 'You know what I'm talking about. You told Emma I had to join you for dinner.'

'I told Emma I thought it was time you fitted into our routine. When I'm home in the evening, I have dinner at eight. And I have it in the dining-room.'

'I prefer eating in my room. I...'

He turned away and lifted a bottle of wine from a table near the doorway. 'If you're going to spend time with my son during the day, I'll want to hear about the things he does and says. You can report to me during dinner.'

Try and argue with that, Rachel told herself. 'Well then, what about my clothes? I wanted my own things.'

'So did your landlord.' His eyebrows rose as he looked across the terrace at her. 'He rented your apartment to someone else, Rachel. You forgot to pay this month's rent. He says your things are in storage in the basement, but he didn't know which boxes contained your clothing, and I couldn't see shipping all of them here.'

Rachel closed her eyes and then opened them again. 'You could have told me that,' she said weakly.

'I didn't know until this afternoon,' he said pleasantly. 'That's when I telephoned Lord & Taylor.'

'And that's another thing. You could have let me pick out my own replacements.'

David's eyes skimmed over her. 'Why? Don't you like the selection?'

She nodded. 'Yes, of course. But I can't afford these things.' A pink blush rose to her cheeks. 'Miss Walters was right, you know. I'd have been better off at Sears'.'

David grinned. 'Vanessa should learn to sheathe her claws,' he said, easing the cork from the bottle. 'Don't worry about affording them—consider them part of the benefits that come with the job.'

She shook her head. 'No, I couldn't.'

He filled two glasses with dark red wine and handed her one. 'Why not? You got them at the Rooster, didn't you? Health care, dental care, whatever.'

Rachel smiled humourlessly. 'The only perks we got at the Rooster were any sandwiches we could scoff at the end of the night.'

'Well then, your employee benefits are better here. Just think of it that way.' David took a sip of wine and then smiled at her across the rim of the glass. 'Does everything fit?'

'I think so. Miss Walters picked all the right sizes. I guess I'll have to thank her.'

David grinned and one dark eyebrow arched upward. 'I'm the one to thank.' His eyes flickered over her again. 'I'm glad to hear I guessed right.'

She thought of the delicate lace underwear beneath the cashmere dress and flushed with embarrassment.

'What kind of wine is this?' she asked quickly. 'I don't think they carry it at the Rooster.'

He laughed. 'No, I'm sure they don't. It's a '59 Burgundy. I brought a case of it back from France last month. Would you like some more?'

Rachel shook her head. 'No, thank you. Wine always goes right to my head.' She leaned her elbows on the stone wall that enclosed the terrace and stared at the darkening mountains. 'Do you do a lot of travelling?'

'More than I sometimes like.' She glanced up at the nearness of his voice, surprised to find that he'd crossed the terrace to stand beside her, his back leaning against the wall as he stared into the dim recesses of the diningroom. 'I hate like hell to leave this place for too long. I've only had it for a couple of years, and it's just beginning to feel like home.'

She thought of the perfectly decorated, lifeless rooms and nodded. 'I guess it takes time to make a house your own. You can tell a decorator what you want, but it doesn't always work.' The impact of what she'd said struck her and she cleared her throat. 'Not that the house isn't magnificent,' she said quickly. 'It is. It really is.'

He shrugged and turned so that they were both gazing out into the evening sky. 'Don't apologise. You're right—the house is too perfect. I guess I lived in dreary hotel rooms and boarding houses too long to know how to turn a house into a home.'

'You?' She laughed in disbelief. 'Dreary hotel rooms?'

'I'm not even sure that describes some of them. The first company I took over was in Pittsburgh. Have you ever been there?' She shook her head and he smiled. 'I had a room in a hotel that could most charitably be described as one step up from a hovel. There was coal dust in every corner of it—even in the air I breathed. God, I'll never forget trying to get that damned dirt out from under my nails!'

'But you did,' she said with a smile.

David nodded. 'It took me half a bar of soap and some skin, but I did. It was a hell of a lot easier than it had been the first time.'

'You said that was the first company you'd taken over.'

'That part of it was new. The coal dust wasn't.' He shifted his weight, turning so that he faced her. 'I was a miner until I was twenty-one, Rachel. Three years in the mines deposits a layer of dirt on a man that never really leaves him.'

Her eyes skimmed his face. 'A miner? But...but you're on Wall Street! They call you a financial genius.'

He laughed softly, enjoying the disbelief he saw registered in her eyes. 'Not every man who's successful on the Street has a degree from Harvard.' A grin tugged at the corners of his mouth. 'I'm not even sure Harvard teaches you how to buy corporations.'

'Neither does working in a coalmine.'

'Yeah,' he sighed, running his fingers through his dark hair, 'that's the truth. God, how I hated it! But there wasn't much choice. When I was eighteen the State said that's it, you're on your own, Griffin. No more State-subsidised foster-homes for you.'

Rachel looked up at him, wondering at the sudden bile in his voice. 'What about the people you lived with? Your foster-parents? Didn't they offer to...'

His teeth flashed whitely in a wolfish grin. 'I know what you're thinking, Rachel. Yeah, I'm sure there are foster-parents who love their kids, but I sure as hell never met any of them. I was just an extra few dollars a month to the ones I stayed with. The State can call them what it likes, but you can't replace a real parent...' He shrugged his shoulders. 'Sorry, I seem to be making speeches tonight.'

He had turned towards the mountains again, his eyes unseeing as they stared at the purple shadows falling on the distant peaks. Rachel looked at his hands as they lay beside hers on the wall, picturing the blunt, well-manicured nails cracked and blackened.

'That's why you came for Jamie, isn't it?' she asked softly. 'To give him a real parent.'

David nodded. 'And to share all this with him,' he said, motioning to the rolling lawn and the mountains beyond. 'You were right when you said that, Rachel. I want him to have the childhood I never had.' His voice hoarsened with suppressed emotion. 'I was so damned determined to do something with my life, to live in a place where you could see the sun and hear laughter... And there I was, trapped in a hole in the ground eight hours a day!'

Her eyes were drawn to the slight crook in his nose and the scar at the corner of his mouth.

'Is that how you got those?' she asked.

He ran his hand along the bridge of his once-broken nose. 'In a mining accident, you mean?' He grinned and shook his head. 'No, not quite. We worked hard and we played hard—hell, it wasn't a bad life when I was eighteen.' Something quickened in his eyes. 'But by the time I was twenty-one, I wanted more.'

'How...what did you do?'

He laughed self-consciously. 'It was what I didn't do that made the difference. I didn't spend my money the way the other men did. Some of them had families to support—I had only myself. Some of them drank or had women...'

Nervous laughter bubbled in Rachel's throat. 'Don't tell me you saved money by becoming celibate!'

He looked down at her and smiled, and she sensed that his mood was lightening.

'I've been pretty fortunate,' he told her. 'I've never had to pay for my women.'

She gave him a quick smile in return. No, she thought, no, I'll bet you haven't. When she spoke, her teasing tone of voice matched his.

'So you saved your money and you bought yourself a corporation. Sounds simple.'

He laughed softly. 'I saved my money, and one night, when I couldn't face that damned boarding house again, I let myself get talked into an all-night poker game.

His arm brushed hers. Rachel looked down at the top of the wall in surprise. He was wearing a jacket and she was wearing the cashmere dress, yet it had felt as if they were skin to skin, the heat from his body almost burning into hers. She moved her arm away from his. The effort for the simple movement seemed enormous. 'I couldn't resist him,' Cassie had said. 'I just couldn't...'

'I see,' she said, forcing a lightness she didn't feel into her voice. 'You won your first corporation.'

'I won five hundred dollars,' he corrected. 'It was more money than I'd ever seen at one time in my life. I was afraid to keep it in my room or in my wallet, so the next day I decided to open a bank account. But on my way to the bank I passed a broker's office. There was a sign out front—I don't even remember what it said. Something about doubling your money through investments. I went in and plunked my five hundred bucks down on some guy's desk. "Put that in something that's gonna make me rich," I said.' He laughed and shook his head at the memory. 'He wrote down five or six suggestions and I closed my eyes and stuck my finger on one. "That's it," I said. "Put it all on that."'

David's voice stilled. In the distance a nightbird called, its cry high and lonely. Rachel shivered involuntarily. 'And? What happened?'

She heard his sudden intake of breath. When he spoke again, his voice was cool and controlled.

'Within a few years, I had a better feel for the market than the broker. And I had a knack for sensing when a company was in trouble and capitalising on it. I learned how to move in and take control, get rid of bad managers and arrange a merger or redistribute the assets.'

Rachel looked up at him. 'You make it sound so...so benevolent,' she said softly.

'I'm not the one who makes them fail, Rachel. I just come on the scene when...'

'...when it's time for the kill,' she said before she could stop herself. 'That's why they call you the Hawk.'

In the gathering dark she could see the gleam of his teeth as he smiled. 'Hawks are like most predators. They kill those things that are simplest to catch—the old, the infirm, the foolish.' He shifted his weight so that his arm lay against hers again. 'I'll have to take you out with me when I fly Isis some time so I can improve your image of hawks, Rachel.'

His hand closed lightly on hers, his fingers curling around hers as they lay on the stone ledge. A tremor ran through her like the almost-heard notes of a finger trailing along the keys of a faraway piano.

'I don't think you can,' she said softly.

David turned towards her, his hand still grasping hers. In the gathering darkness he was only a ghostly figure, but she could see the glint of his feral eyes, smell his scent, hear his breathing.

'It's getting dark,' she said quickly. 'Shouldn't we go inside? Dinner must be ready.'

'Hawks aren't one-dimensional creatures, Rachel,' he said in a soft whisper. 'And most people know very little about them.'

'That's true,' she said nervously.

His other hand touched her shoulder, the lean fingers spreading over the soft cashmere.

'Does that mean you'd like to learn more about hawks?'

'No,' she said quickly, wishing the moon would rise so she could see his face, 'no, not really.'

'Ah, but you should.' He moved closer to her. 'After all, my hawks will be part of Jamie's existence. Suppose he asks you questions about them?'

Sweet relief flooded through her. 'Will I be here that long?'

David said nothing. His hand moved from her shoulder to her throat, and his thumb pressed lightly in the shadowed hollow where her pulse beat. Could he feel the leap of her blood beneath his fingers? she wondered.

'Rachel...'

His voice was thick. She swallowed with difficulty and tried to step back from him, but her feet seemed rooted to the floor.

'David,' she began, 'listen...'

'I love the way you say my name,' he whispered as his hand threaded through the hair at the nape of her neck. 'Say it again, Rachel.'

Panic danced along her spine. 'David, please...'

His head lowered towards hers. 'Please what?' he murmured, his breath warm and fresh against her face. 'Tell me, Rachel...tell me what you want me to do.' He brought her hand up between them, flattening her palm against his chest. The rapid thud of his heart hammered beneath her fingers. 'Do you feel that? That's what you do to me.'

She closed her eyes, willing herself to remember who he was, who she was. *Help me, Cassie...*

'Stop!' she begged. 'David...'

'You don't mean that,' he said. 'I know you don't.'

'Yes,' she said desperately, 'yes, I do, I...'

She gasped as his hand covered her breast, lying lightly against the soft wool and the softer flesh beneath.

'No, you don't,' he said huskily. 'Your heart is racing, Rachel. You want me as much as I want you.' His hand swept behind her, to the small of her back, and he brought her body against his. 'Tell me,' he demanded. 'Say it!'

His body, hard and aroused, pressed against her. Rachel's lashes fell, her eyelids closed. She felt she was on fire. Every nerve ending, every inch of skin was burning, hungering...

Light blazed suddenly in the dining-room. The terrace door slammed and Rachel pushed free of David's encircling arms. In the darkness, Emma's voice was a bodiless reminder of reality.

'Mr Griffin? Sir, I'm sorry to bother you, but Jamie's crying. It's not serious; I think he's just cutting a tooth. But it would calm him if Miss Cooper went up to see him.'

David nodded. 'We'll both go.'

Rachel closed her eyes as he pushed past her. Thank you, Jamie, she thought. He had given her a reprieve—although something told her it would be brief.

CHAPTER SIX

RACHEL stepped slowly down the curving staircase, moving quietly in the early morning silence. The sun, streaming through the skylight in the entry foyer, touched the green plants and glass tables with gold. It was just past seven. Jamie was sound asleep in his crib, exhausted after a long night of tears and tooth-cutting. Rachel was exhausted, too, but she'd spent enough nights like this one to know that climbing into bed and pulling the covers over her head now would only make her sluggish and irritable. A couple of hours' sleep and a cool shower had made her feel almost human. A pot of strong coffee and some eggs would probably do the rest.

Emma had got to the kitchen first, she thought, sniffing appreciatively. Coffee...and bacon. Toast, too. Her stomach growled in anticipation as she pushed against the swinging door.

'Good morning, Emma. I'd have thought you'd still be asleep...'

She broke off in confusion as David grinned at her from across the room. 'She is,' he said. 'So should you be. It was a long night.' He was standing at the stove barefoot, dressed in running shorts and a white tee-shirt that clung to him like a second skin. His dark hair was as damp as hers and he ran a self-conscious hand through it as she looked at him. 'I ran a couple of miles to wake myself up, and when I got back, I was ravenous!'

The bacon sizzled on the griddle behind him. David turned and forked several crisp strips from the pan, laying them on the counter to drain. Rachel's eyes followed the play of muscle across his shoulders, the flesh moulded and defined by the close-fitting cotton shirt.

'Yes, I know,' she said slowly. 'That's why I came downstairs. I thought I'd make myself some breakfast.' She glanced at the table set for one and then at David again. The large, airy room seemed suddenly too small for them both. 'Look, I can come back later...'

'For God's sake, Rachel, don't be silly. There's more than enough here.' He turned back to the stove and expertly flipped over a row of golden-brown pancakes. 'Go on, get yourself a cup and have some coffee,' he said, motioning her to the table with a sweep of the spatula.

The aroma of the coffee and the bacon flooded her senses. With a sigh of resignation, she set a place for herself and then slipped into a chair. 'I thought I'd have the kitchen to myself,' she said, filling her cup with coffee. 'I mean, Emma must be exhausted. And I never expected to find you here.'

He turned off the stove and smiled at her. 'Do I look that out of place? I admit, I haven't made these in a long time, but I used to be pretty good in the kitchen. How's the coffee? Too strong?'

'No, no, it's fine. It's just what I needed. I think we were up half the night.'

David loaded two plates with pancakes and bacon and set them on the table. 'My son didn't give us much choice,' he said in a voice filled with pride. 'Two teeth at once—I'll bet that's some kind of record!' He grinned and pushed her plate towards her. 'Go on, Rachel, dig in. Emma would never forgive me if I let you starve.' He slipped into a chair opposite her, watching as she poured maple syrup on her pancakes and cut into them. 'Well?' he demanded as she chewed her first mouthful. 'How are they?'

Surprise lit her face. 'They're really good.'

David smiled. 'The Lindy recipe,' he said mysteriously.

Rachel laughed. 'Ah, I see. Handed down in secret over the generations, right?'

He shook his head and smiled. 'Handed down in seven months of watching Mrs Lindy make pancakes on a coal stove in the Monongahela Valley.'

'A coal stove?'

He nodded. 'The twentieth century is still creeping up on some parts of the world, Rachel. The Lindys had a clapboard house with an outdoor privy and a coal stove. Six days a week, Mrs Lindy cooked porridge on that stove for breakfast, the same lumpy porridge I'd been gagging over as far back as I could remember. But on Sundays...' He sighed and the expression on his face became wistful. 'On Sundays, she always made pancakes. Flapjacks, she called them. I can still close my eyes and smell them.'

'And?' Rachel prompted gently. 'Did she teach you to make her flapjacks?'

His teeth flashed whitely. 'Mr Lindy probably would have hung her from the nearest tree! Men didn't cook in the Monongahela Valley, at least not then, they didn't. No, I just watched. There used to be something special about those mornings. She in her robe, he in the oldest slippers I've ever seen...' He cleared his throat and reached for the coffee pot. 'Listen, don't pay any attention to me. I talk too much when I haven't had enough sleep.'

She watched him as he refilled their cups. 'How old were you then?'

He shrugged his shoulders. 'Almost fourteen. Old enough to have known it wouldn't last.'

Rachel sighed and wrapped her hands around her coffee cup. 'That's a rough age,' she remarked. 'You're not old enough to be an adult and not young enough to be a child. Cassie was fourteen when our parents...' She looked up at him and then back at the table. 'About the clothes you bought me, David—I'd like to make some arrangements to repay you.'

He shook his head. 'Fringe benefits, remember? What were you saying about Cassie? What happened to your parents?'

She took a deep breath and let it out slowly. 'They died,' she said finally, laying her fork across her plate. 'They were on vacation in Colorado and there was a flash flood. They were driving across a bridge and it washed out.'

David sat back in his chair, his cup raised to his lips. 'That must have been awful,' he said softly.

Rachel nodded. 'It was,' she said simply. 'I'd just finished high school—they said they'd never had a proper honeymoon and that now I was old enough to take care of Cassie...' Her eyes darkened with long-forgotten memories. 'That really wasn't anything new, of course. I'd been responsible for Cassie for a long time. Ever since my mother married her father...' She looked across the table at him. 'You know all those stories about wicked step-parents?' she asked. David nodded. 'Well, none of them were true for me. Our parents really loved each other. They never seemed to need anybody else.'

'Nobody?' His eyebrows rose. 'Didn't that make you feel left out?'

Her face flushed and she looked at him in surprise. 'No,' she said quickly, 'of course not. I had Cassie.'

'You had Cassie,' he repeated, sitting back in his chair. 'You were, what, three years older than she?'

'Four,' she said, 'I was four years older than Cassie. And I loved her a lot,' she added with sudden defiance.

His eyes narrowed, the gold-flecked irises seeming to darken. 'Yes, I'm sure you did, Rachel. Did she love you too?'

'What's that supposed to mean? Of course she did. Why wouldn't she?'

He shrugged. 'I was just wondering. You seem so different.'

'Look,' she said, pushing her chair back from the table, 'this has nothing to do with anything. I...'

'Was Cassie as good with Jamie as you are?'

Colour rose to her cheeks. 'She was his mother.'

'That's not what I asked.'

'Of course she was good with him,' she said quickly.

'Funny—I wouldn't have thought so. She struck me as too self-centred, too...'

'You didn't know her very well, then,' Rachel snapped.

David's eyes caught hers. 'That's certainly the truth,' he said softly.

'Cassie was as sweet as she was beautiful. When we were little...'

'What about when you were grown up?'

'Nothing changed,' she said, then her eyes met his. 'She was very busy,' she said quickly. 'But that was to be expected. She had her career.'

'How old were you when your mother married her father?'

'Why all these questions?' she demanded. 'None of this has anything to do with Jamie.'

David pushed his plate aside. 'Does it bother you to talk about your childhood?'

Rachel stared at him. 'Do you always answer a question with a question?'

He grinned and shrugged his shoulders. 'Let's just say I'm trying to learn all I can about Jamie.'

Rachel sighed. It was hard to argue with that. 'I was twelve when they married,' she told him.

'Just beginning to think about boys and dates?'

She shook her head. 'That was Cassie when she got to be twelve. No, I was gawky and shy at that age. Cassie was eight, and she was beautiful. All blonde curls and creamy skin—everybody loved her. I used to wish my grandmother had lived long enough to have known her.'

He smiled. 'The same grandmother you like to quote?'

Rachel nodded. 'She lived with us when I was a baby, after my real father's death. I missed her terribly when she died.'

'But then Cassie came along.'

She smiled at the memory. 'Yes, then Cassie came along. And I had my very own little sister to love and care for.'

David's voice was gentle. 'And who loved *you*?'

'My mother, of course, and my stepfather. And Cassie.'

She had a sudden image of her parents seated close together, laughing softly at a private joke while a golden-haired Cassie looked out of the window, waiting for one of her boyfriends to arrive.

Jamie, she thought, that's who I had, that's all I ever really had. To her chagrin, tears stung her eyes. Quickly she shoved her chair towards the table and picked up her dishes.

'Thanks for breakfast. I...'

But he was beside her before she could move, his hand grasping her shoulder. 'Rachel, I'm sorry, I didn't mean to make you cry.'

'You didn't,' she said quickly. 'I'm...I'm just overtired.'

'I know how much Jamie means to you. And I'm grateful for all you've done.'

'Dammit, I don't want your gratitude—I want...'

'I know what you want,' he said slowly. 'You want Jamie. And I understand it—now.'

Of course he did, she thought. The sense of obligation that had driven him to take his son from her had been replaced by love for the child. The realisation didn't surprise her. Despite what the papers said, despite what

Cassie had said, there was a side to him that was tender and giving. Sometimes it was hard to realise that the David Griffin who had used her stepsister so carelessly was the David Griffin she'd come to know. But he was. He was...

'Rachel?' He said her name softly, leaning closer to her.

'I...I think I'll go to my room now,' she murmured. 'It's getting late.'

'It's not even eight o'clock!'

'Then I'll check on Jamie.'

'Emma's sleeping in the nursery.' David took a strand of her hair in his fingers, letting the dark curl loop softly around his hand. 'Why do you keep running from me, Rachel?'

She swallowed drily. 'I don't. I...'

'You have to learn not to run,' he said softly. 'All it does is draw attention. Even a rabbit knows that.'

There was a thread of warning in the simple words. Her eyes lifted to his, and she thought suddenly that she knew how the rabbit felt under the fierce gaze of the hawk. Rachel tore her eyes from his face and looked downward in confusion. His shirt was V-necked; she could see the pulse beating in the hollow of his throat. Dark tendrils of hair curled above the V. His hand slid to her throat, his fingers touching her lightly, their callused strength stroking lazy patterns on her skin.

'David...' She put her hand on his forearm and suddenly she remembered how it had felt to have his arms around her. Her breath quickened and she pulled away from him. 'Don't...don't you have to leave for work?' It was trite, but it was all she could think of.

The sound of his laughter was throaty and intimate, as if he knew what she'd been thinking.

'That's the nicest part of being your own boss—you make your own hours. I'm taking today off.' He grinned and touched his index finger to the tip of her nose. 'This is a red letter day, Rachel. My son has two brand new teeth, remember?'

Relief flooded through her at the change in their conversation and she laughed softly.

'Of course. Well, what'll it be? A party at the Waldorf? A twenty-one gun salute?'

'Go on, woman, tease me all you like. When my son does something...'

'All babies get teeth, David,' she said gently.

'Teeth like those? And two at once?' He laughed and turned her towards the doorway. 'Come on, get into your city best. We're going to buy that boy a present.'

'But what could he possibly need? You've already given him everything.'

'We're not going to get him something he needs, we're going to get him something special. And I know just the place to find it.'

Two hours later, Rachel had given up asking David where they were going. 'Is this it?' she had asked as the Jaguar approached a shopping centre.

'No,' he had said mysteriously. 'Not this one.'

After she had got the same answer six times, she had sighed and resigned herself to watching the landscape whizz by. All she was certain of was that they were heading south. Twisting mountain roads gave way to the houses of suburbia, and finally she could see the towers of New York City rising in the distance.

'All this for a toy store?' she asked.

David flashed her a quick smile. 'This isn't just a toy store. It's Mecca for kids. Just wait until you see it!'

By the time they reached Manhattan, she was sure she knew where they were going. The man was crazy, she told herself as they drove up Fifth Avenue, but nicely so.

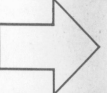

NO COST! NO OBLIGATION TO BUY! NO PURCHASE NECESSARY!

PLAY "LUCKY 7"
AND GET AS MANY AS SIX FREE GIFTS...

HOW TO PLAY:

1. With a coin, carefully scratch off the silver box at the right. This makes you eligible to receive one or more free books, and possibly other gifts, depending on what is revealed beneath the scatch-off area.

2. You'll receive brand-new Presents® novels. When you return this card, we'll send you the books and gifts you qualify for absolutely free!

3. Unless you tell us otherwise, every month we'll send you 8 additional novels to read and enjoy. If you decide to keep them, you'll pay only $1.99 per book*, a savings of 26¢ per book. There is no extra charge for postage and handling. There are no hidden extras.

4. When you join Harlequin Reader Service, we'll send you additional free gifts from time to time, as well as our newsletter.

5. You must be completely satisfied. You may cancel at any time just by dropping us a line or returning a shipment of books at our cost.

* Terms and prices subject to change.

DETACH AND MAIL CARD TODAY

BUSINESS REPLY CARD

First Class   Permit No. 717   Buffalo, NY

Postage will be paid by addressee

Harlequin Reader Service®
901 Fuhrmann Blvd.,
P.O. Box 1867
Buffalo, NY 14240-9952

NO POSTAGE
NECESSARY
IF MAILED
IN THE
UNITED STATES

'We're going to FAO Schwarz, aren't we?' she asked.

David grinned at her. 'Absolutely. Have you been there?'

She shook her head. 'It's too expensive for me, but I know about it. Everybody in New York knows about it.'

'Then you're long overdue for a visit. I guarantee that you'll feel as if you were a kid again inside of ten minutes!'

For a fleeting instant, Rachel wondered whether she'd lost her mind. Here she was, seated alongside David Griffin, laughing and talking with him as if they were friends and not adversaries. But there was no time to think. He was hurrying her into the store, tugging her after him towards what looked like a teddy-bear convention. And within minutes, all her efforts were concentrated on the merits of talking bears versus plain, huggable teddies. And then, of course, there were brown bears as opposed to white bears, and it wasn't easy to decide whether big ones were better than little ones...

Finally Rachel surrendered. 'Go on, David, buy all of them. We'll give Jamie one bear a day for a week, then he'll have his own bear pack.'

David laughed. 'The perfect solution! You heard the lady,' he said to the salesman. 'We'll take them all. Gift-wrapped, of course.'

The salesman smiled. 'Of course, sir. Will there be anything else?'

'Yes,' said David, taking Rachel's arm. 'We need a...what do we need, Rachel? A train? A new set of blocks? Finger paints?'

She looked up at him and shook her head. 'Are you joking? You just bought Jamie a dozen stuffed animals!'

'Seven,' he said modestly.

'And you want to buy something else? David, you'll spoil him!'

'Babies can't be spoiled,' he said, 'only loved. Didn't anybody ever tell you that? Besides, you haven't got him anything yet. What do you think he'd like? Trains? Yes, sure, every boy has to have a set of trains. But which kind? Wooden? Electric?'

Rachel sighed in defeat. 'Wooden ones. He's only a year old.'

David nodded solemnly. 'See? It's a good thing you came with me. What do I know about babies?' He turned to the salesman who had followed them at a discreet distance. 'Trains,' he said. 'Wooden ones. Well, electric ones, too. He'll grow into them,' he added before Rachel could protest. 'Kids his age grow fast.'

She had to laugh. It was like watching a child turned loose in a candy store! David directed the salesman from one end of the store to the other. Blocks, soldiers, cars, trucks—the toys piled up before them, an assortment large enough to keep a dozen children busy for years. David's own delight in all of them was infectious. He wound things up and watched them go with a childish pleasure that made people around them smile, and Rachel found herself imagining the bleak emptiness of his own childhood. What a lonely little boy he must have been... She stepped forward at last and put her hand on his arm.

'David,' she said gently, 'really, that's enough. Jamie will never be able to play with all that.'

He looked at the stacks of toys and flashed her an embarrassed smile. 'I guess I went overboard, huh?' he said, raking his fingers through his hair. 'OK, no more for today. I'd like these delivered, please.'

The salesman nodded. 'Certainly, sir. And may I say your son is very fortunate to have such a loving mother and father.'

Rachel shook her head. 'Oh, but we're not...' The explanation caught in her throat.

David's hand closed over hers. 'Thank you,' he said. 'We do, indeed, love our boy. Don't we, Rachel?'

She was afraid to answer. She nodded instead and then turned and headed blindly for the door, David's voice echoing hollowly in her ears.

'Rachel? Rachel, wait...'

'I want to go back now, David,' she said stiffly, standing on the pavement. 'It's getting late.'

'Look, the guy didn't mean anything...'

'I want to go back to the house,' she repeated.

'He just made a natural assumption...'

She brushed the tears from her eyes. 'Drop it, please.'

'Dammit, Rachel, why are you crying?'

White-faced, she swung around to face him, oblivious to the hurrying pedestrians swirling past.

'Because I just remembered that I have to give Jamie up,' she said fiercely. 'That's why.'

David nodded slowly. 'Yes, I've been thinking about that.'

There was a prickle of fear on her spine. 'What does that mean?' she whispered.

He shrugged. 'We can't talk about it here,' he said.

Desperation quickened her voice. 'You said I could stay for a few months. You said...'

'I know what I said, Rachel. But it isn't working out the way I'd planned.'

So, she thought, there it was. First the carrot, then the stick. This was where he'd been heading all along. You didn't just turn down a man like David Griffin. He'd proved that with Cassie.

'No,' she said finally. 'I bet it hasn't.'

'It hasn't. I expected...'

She laughed unpleasantly. 'What now, David? Do I get showered with jewels and flowers? Or will it be something else? Do you just dangle Jamie over my head? I'm not Cassie—you can't use the same methods.'

'What the hell are you talking about?'

'Come on, David, I'm not that dumb. A little naïve, maybe, but I saw what happened to Cassie. I understand.'

His hands, like claws, shot out and grasped her shoulders. 'For God's sake, Rachel, Cassie has nothing to do with this!'

'She has everything to do with it,' she said in a furious whisper.

'You know something?' he growled, pulling her towards him. 'You're right—she does. And we're going to settle this once and for all. Or are you going to try running away from me again? You do it each time.'

'If only Cassie had run,' she snapped. 'But no, she wouldn't have, not from a man like you. She never learned, no matter what I said. But I'm not like her— and you just can't handle that, can you? You...'

David smiled grimly as her words trailed off into silence. 'So,' he said softly, 'you do know what she really was like.'

Rachel shook her head in useless denial. 'No,' she said quickly, 'no, she was my baby sister. She... What are you doing?'

'We're going somewhere with a little more privacy,' he said, catching her wrist in a grip of steel. 'Even New Yorkers can't resist a free show like this.'

Rachel looked around her, suddenly aware of the ring of curious faces that surrounded them.

'No,' she said. 'I...' But her protests were useless. 'David,' she panted, tripping along beside him, 'where are you taking me?'

'I told you,' he said, pulling her after him. 'Somewhere where we can be alone. We're going to talk about Cassie.'

'I know all I need to know.'

'Yes,' he said grimly, 'I think you do. I'm just going to make sure you face it.'

A doorway loomed before her, the doorman's startled face a blur.

'Evening, Mr Griffin. Nice weather.'

David mumbled something as he propelled Rachel through an elegant lobby and into an elevator. Her eyes met those of the elevator operator and she flushed and looked away. When they reached the top floor, David stepped into the hall and tugged her after him.

'Let go of me!' she demanded as the elevator door hissed shut.

His hand dropped from her wrist. 'Get inside,' he said flatly as he unlocked the door before them. 'Get yourself comfortable and sit down.'

Twilight shadows muted the colours of a large sitting-room. Rachel stood watching sullenly as David pulled off his jacket and tossed it on to a white brocade couch.

'Brandy or cognac?' he demanded, stalking to a bar across the room.

'I want to know where we are,' she said, rubbing her chafed wrist. 'You...you can't just kidnap somebody...'

'Cognac,' he said, making the decision for her. He handed her a brandy glass with a dark liquid swirling in its crystal depths. 'Sit down, Rachel.'

'Did you hear me? I want some answers!'

'This is my apartment. I use it when I'm stuck in town. Any other questions?'

'Yes,' she snapped. 'What are we doing here?'

'I already told you that. We're going to talk about Cassie.'

'We're not! She was...'

'She was your stepsister. And you loved her—I know that. But I'm tired of having her stand between us.'

Rachel tossed her head. 'There is no "us", David. I...' She took a hurried step back as he crossed the room and took the glass from her hand. 'Don't,' she said quickly, 'please...'

His arms closed around her and his mouth came down on hers with a punishing ferocity. The kiss lasted for only a heartbeat, but it left her trembling and shaken.

'Go on,' he growled, 'tell me again that there's no "us".' He waited while she stared helplessly into his eyes, then he smiled grimly. 'Sit down, Rachel.'

She took the drink from him and moved slowly backwards until she felt the couch behind her.

'What do you want from me?' she whispered as she sank to the cushion.

'I want you to face the truth,' he said. 'I want you to admit that I didn't rape your stepsister...'

'I never said you raped her, for God's sake!'

'...and I didn't get her drunk or kidnap her or dazzle her with jewels, Rachel. We were together, yes, but...'

Rachel held up her hand. 'Please,' she whispered, 'spare me the details.'

'It didn't mean a damned thing,' he growled. 'It was just an encounter.'

Her eyes closed in pain. 'Don't,' she begged. 'Don't make it worse than it is.'

David sat on the couch beside her. 'What did she tell you, Rachel?' he asked softly. 'Did she say we were lovers? We weren't. We were just two people who came together one night.'

'One night? You took her away for a weekend, David. You...you spent weeks trying to seduce her, and then you...you turned your back on her when she told you she was pregnant.' Rachel's voice broke and she covered her face. 'I don't want to talk about it,' she said brokenly. 'I beg you...'

She felt his hands close on hers. Gently, determinedly, he drew her hands from her face and clasped them in his.

'Listen to me, Rachel,' he said slowly. 'There was no seduction. There wasn't even a weekend. We met at a party. She was with someone else—but she came on to me anyway. She phoned me the next day. She asked me to lunch or dinner or something and I turned her down.'

Rachel shook her head. 'No. You called her. You...'

His fingers laced through hers. 'She kept calling my office. Finally I took her out for an evening. We had nothing to say to each other. We went to dinner, to the theatre, and I took her home and that was the end of it. Until almost two years ago—I was at a hotel on Martinique. I'd gone there on business and... well, it doesn't matter. Cassie was there with a man. I saw them in the bar, quarrelling about something. He left and she came to me. She was pretty drunk, Rachel—she said... she said some things... Anyway, I saw her to her room, went back to the bar for another drink, and then I called it a night. In the early hours of the morning I awakened and she was in my room, standing there beside my bed, naked, smiling at me.' He broke off and closed his eyes. 'I should have thrown her out, but she was beautiful, and exciting. And...'

Rachel pulled her hands from his. 'No,' she whispered.

'Yes,' he said flatly. 'She was gone when I woke in the morning, and I never saw her again until she came to my office and claimed to be carrying my child.'

Rachel's face contorted with pain. 'Cassie was... was a free spirit, yes. But what you're describing—David, she wasn't like that. She...'

'She was exactly like that.' He grasped her shoulders and forced her to face him. 'Stop lying to yourself, Rachel. She went from man to man—everybody knew it. And when she said she was pregnant—well, she wasn't the first woman who'd tried to pull something like that on a rich man. After all, there'd only been that one time... For all I know, it was just a lucky guess on her part.'

Rachel shuddered. 'No, it isn't true. She was spoiled, yes, I knew that. She always had been. And it was hard for her when our parents died. She was only fourteen...' She took a breath and her eyes sought David's. 'If you felt this way about her—if all this is true, then why...why did you suddenly come forward after...after...'

'After she overdosed? I told you why. Because of Jamie. He had no one. I thought of my own childhood.' He laid his palm against her cheek and gently raised her face. 'It wasn't my intention to hurt your stepsister, Rachel,' he said softly. 'You must believe me.'

Rachel swallowed. 'I... David, I'm so confused. I...I don't know what to think.'

'I've told you the truth, Rachel. I can't do anything more than that. I'm not proud of my part in it, but I'm not the villain Cassie made me out to be. I want you to know that.'

Bitter laughter welled in her throat. 'The worst of this is that I want to believe you.'

David's golden eyes met hers. 'Do you?'

Rachel nodded. 'I'm ashamed to admit it. But I...I'd rather think my stepsister was...that she... I'd rather believe that than think you used her and then tossed her aside.'

David's hands slid to her arms. 'Rachel,' he said thickly, 'Rachel...'

She shook her head and drew back. 'No,' she said quickly, 'don't.'

'Rachel, I...'

She closed her eyes and her voice dropped to a whisper. 'Please,' she sighed, 'take me home.'

'You must believe me,' he said softly.

'I...I don't know what to believe.'

He bent forward and his lips brushed hers in a light kiss. 'Yes,' he said in a husky whisper, 'yes, you do.'

No, she thought later, watching him from under lowered lashes as the car sped through the night, no, she didn't know what to believe. She knew what she wanted to believe. And that wasn't necessarily the same thing at all.

CHAPTER SEVEN

RACHEL sat in the kitchen the next morning, her hands locked around a cup of coffee that was growing cooler by the minute when the door swung open. She looked up and her eyes met David's.

'Good morning,' he said softly.

'Good morning,' she replied. 'There's fresh coffee. Would you like some?'

He smiled as he sat down. 'Thanks, yes, I'd love some. Where's Emma?'

Rachel arose and took a cup and saucer from the cabinet. 'She took Jamie for shoes. Now that he's begun walking, we decided it was time to put something substantial on his feet.' She filled the cup and put it on the table. 'I don't know how you take your coffee, David. With cream and sugar?'

'Black, no sugar is fine.' He lifted the cup to his lips, watching her through the rising steam from the dark liquid. 'I'm surprised you didn't go with her.'

A light flush rose to her cheeks as she sat down again. 'I am too,' she admitted with a hesitant laugh. 'But I was up half the night...'

'Yes, I was too. Rachel, I'm sorry for what happened. Maybe I shouldn't have told you those things. Maybe...'

She shook her head. 'No, no, I'm glad you did. It makes things easier to understand.'

'About Cassie?'

She nodded. 'And about myself.' Her voice dropped to an embarrassed whisper. 'What I'm trying to say is that you aren't really the way I thought you'd be. Cassie painted you differently. And now that you've told me—now that you've told me how...what happened, I...'

David reached across the table and laid his hand on hers. 'You believe me, then,' he said quietly.

Her eyes lifted and met his. 'I want to,' she admitted.

His voice was gentle. 'You loved your stepsister very much, didn't you?'

Rachel nodded again. 'Yes, I did. I told you how I felt when our parents married—it was as if someone had given me a live doll to fuss over. And Cassie loved being fussed over. She was so pretty, David, with her blonde hair and blue eyes... And then, when our folks died in that accident, I became responsible for her.'

'That must have been difficult. You were really only a child yourself.'

She sighed and shrugged her shoulders. 'It was OK for a while. I took a secretarial job and there was some insurance money to keep us going. But Cassie...Cassie got wilder and wilder. I couldn't handle her. When she was eighteen, she moved out.'

David's hand clasped hers more tightly. 'You don't have to tell me all this if it upsets you,' he said quietly.

'No, I want to tell you. I...I don't want you to think badly of Cassie, David. It wasn't her fault that she was...well, that she was the way she was. Sometimes I think she was just too beautiful for her own good. She...'

'Not as beautiful as you, Rachel.'

She looked up at him in surprise, the colour rising to her cheeks again. 'Me? I'm not beautiful.'

He smiled at her. 'Yes, you are. There's an innocence about you, an openness... Even in that horrible costume you wore at the Golden Rooster, you looked like a little girl.'

'Not too little, David. There are laws against child molesting.' Rachel pulled her hand from David's and stumbled to her feet. Vanessa Walters lounged in the doorway, a brilliant smile on her face. 'I hope I didn't interrupt anything,' she said. 'You did ask me to bring the outline for your speech this morning, didn't you?'

David got to his feet and shook his head. 'I didn't expect you this early, Vanessa. Would you like some coffee?'

The woman smiled. 'That's a lovely idea. I take sugar in mine,' she said to Rachel. 'And a piece of toast, if you have it.'

Her presumptuousness made Rachel flush, but David seemed unaware of the byplay. He pulled his chair closer to Vanessa's and peered over her shoulder at a sheaf of papers she'd spread on the table. Rachel poured the coffee and buttered the toast while the two murmured together. An unreasonable irritation mounted within her. She wiped her hands on a towel and tossed it on the counter.

'I'll be upstairs.'

David looked up in surprise. 'Don't go, Rachel. I'm sorry we were so rude, but this had to be taken care of this morning.'

'Let her go, David. She'd be bored to tears.' Vanessa looked at Rachel and smiled politely. 'You probably have things to do, Rachel. There are so many things to keep one busy around a baby, aren't there? Nappies to fold and toys to put away...'

Rachel bit back her anger. 'That's true,' she said evenly. 'Nothing as important as business.'

The woman smiled. 'This is even more important. Didn't Mr Griffin tell you? He's making a speech this evening.'

'It's not a speech, Vanessa,' David said impatiently. 'I'm just accepting an award.'

Vanessa patted his hand. 'Why so modest, David? Surely your son's companion is entitled to know that the

Community Leadership Program has named you man of the year.'

David shrugged. 'It's flattering, but it's not as important as you make it sound.'

The Walters woman clucked her tongue. 'It's as important as we choose to make it. There'll be press coverage—I've even had promises from some television people. Public image is vital, David—you know that.'

He ran his hand through his hair, raking it back from his forehead. 'Yes, I know. But...'

'David, please—trust me. You've got years of sharp edges to smooth away before people start thinking of you as a man instead of a corporate raider. You've taken the first steps—don't get impatient now. Everything's on schedule. By next month...'

David pushed back his chair and got to his feet. 'You were right,' he said sharply. 'I'm afraid we *have* been boring Rachel with all this talk. Will you be at the awards presentation tonight, Vanessa?'

Vanessa's eyes slid to Rachel. 'Of course, if you want me to.'

He nodded. 'I'll see you then.'

She turned a dazzling smile on Rachel. 'You can watch Mr Griffin's acceptance speech on the eleven o'clock news. You do stay up that late, don't you?'

Rachel gritted her teeth. 'Oh, yes,' she said sweetly. 'My coach doesn't turn into a pumpkin until midnight.'

She turned on her heel and stalked out of the kitchen. Vanessa's laughter, mingled with David's low, irritated voice, echoed behind her.

'Rachel, wait...' He caught up with her at the foot of the steps and grasped her by the shoulders. 'She didn't mean that the way it sounded.'

'Yes, she did,' she said with resignation. 'Not that it matters—I don't like her any more than she likes me. She thinks I'm naïve...'

He smiled at her. 'She thinks you're an innocent. It's a quality she doesn't understand.' He reached out and smoothed an errant strand of hair from her cheek, his hand lingering against her skin. 'Are you usually as old-fashioned as you seem?' he asked softly. 'Sometimes I think you've stepped out of another age.'

His eyes were burning with golden intensity. He moved closer to her and she ran her tongue nervously across her lips.

'I'm not that old-fashioned,' she said with forced lightness. 'I can work an electric can-opener and a television set...'

'Has there ever been someone special in your life?'

Her eyes lifted to his. 'No,' she said.

His smile seemed to burn into her soul. 'I'm glad.'

The air around them was charged, thick with tension that made it almost unbreatheable. Rachel moved back a step.

'Don't you... don't you have to get back to Vanessa?'

He smiled and shook his head. 'She's gone. She asked me to give you her apology.'

Rachel made a face. 'I bet!'

'She did,' he insisted, and then he spread his hands and grinned. 'Come on, Rachel. "To err is human, to forgive, divine." Isn't that what Grandma would have said?'

She laughed softly. 'Oh, she'd have loved you, David. You're just like she was. You have an answer for everything.'

His fingers kneaded her shoulders gently. 'Not everything. I'm still waiting to hear why you didn't go with Emma today.'

The confusion that had tormented Rachel in the dark hours before dawn was mirrored in her eyes. She had told herself she wanted to be alone with him so that she could talk to him about Cassie, but now that he was near her, she knew that was only part of the truth. What she really wanted was to be alone with him, to talk and laugh without memories of Cassie punishing her. But her stepsister's ghost had been replaced by a flesh-and-blood intruder. She took a deep breath.

'I just wanted the chance to talk to you, I guess. I . . . I wanted to tell you that . . . that . . .'

She swallowed drily. David put his hand under her chin and lifted her face to his.

'That what?' he prompted softly.

Rachel's heart thudded against her ribs. She drew a breath again and gathered her courage.

'I wanted to tell you that I'm not sorry you and Cassie . . . If you hadn't, I wouldn't have Jamie. And . . . and . . .'

'And we wouldn't have met,' he said, smiling into her eyes. 'Both those possibilities occurred to me too.' His fingers curled around her chin and his golden gaze darkened. 'Rachel?' His voice was soft.

'Yes?' she murmured.

'Can you ride a horse? Do you know how?'

Her eyes widened in astonishment. 'Can I what? Yes, I can ride. Well, I used to, a long time ago, when I could afford it . . . David, what are you doing?' she demanded as he propelled her out of the doorway. 'Where are you taking me? I have to fold Jamie's laundry.'

'Aha! Vanessa was right—you do lead an exciting life.' He feinted to the left and laughed as she aimed a punch at his ribs. 'Leave the laundry for Emma,' he said. 'This is better, believe me.'

'This is better?' Rachel asked breathlessly half an hour later. She was seated on a roan mare, watching David warily as he sat on the black stallion, Isis balanced on his leather-gloved fist. 'Better than what? David, I don't really like that hawk ...'

'You don't know her,' he said softly. 'Give yourself a chance, Rachel. Give her a chance. That's fair, isn't it?'

Rachel sighed. 'Yes,' she admitted, 'I guess so. But I don't want to watch her kill something.'

'She won't. She's accustomed to being hand-fed after a flight. I don't fly her for the kill—that's not what falconry's all about. I fly her to watch her take the sky, to share that moment of freedom with her.' He stopped in mid-sentence and gave Rachel an embarrassed grin. 'Instead of telling you, why don't I just show you?' He looked around them and drew in on the stallion's reins. 'This is a good spot,' he added as he dismounted.

Rachel slid from the roan's back. 'Shall I tie Abdullah to a tree for you?' she asked.

David shook his head. 'He won't wander. But maybe you'd better loop the roan's reins around something— that's it. No sudden moves, now, Rachel. Isis startles easily.' He bent his head towards the hawk and whispered softly to her.

'What are you telling her?'

He grinned. 'I told her to put on the performance of her life. I reminded her that the reputation of the ancient and honourable sport of falconry is hers to defend today. I told her ...'

'All right, all right, I get the idea,' laughed Rachel. 'You want me to change my mind about hawks. Well, I'll watch whatever it is she does. But I'm not promising anything. She's a predator, David. A killer. A ...'

'Watch!' he said.

He bent his head to the hawk, his teeth flashing whitely as he bit open the laces of the hood. Suddenly Isis was in the air, her powerful wings beating rapidly as she climbed into the sky. David stood watching her, his head thrown back, a rapturous smile on his face as he followed her flight.

'Just look at her,' he whispered. 'She hasn't flown in days—and she loves to take to the sky. She'll climb and climb...'

The hawk was high overhead, a dark, streamlined body sailing over the meadow. Rachel could still see the muscular beat of her wings. Suddenly a thin cry echoed on the stillness, and goosebumps rose on Rachel's arms.

'What was that?' she whispered.

David looked at her and smiled. 'That was Isis,' he said. 'She always gives voice when she's happy.'

Rachel shuddered. 'That eerie sound means she's happy?'

He smiled and slid a comforting arm around her waist. 'It's a marvellous sound. It means she's free. When I first got her—when I was manning her, teaching her not to be afraid of me—she never gave voice. But when I finally flew her—hell, I still remember that day, Rachel. I took her out here and talked to her and stroked her and told her how much she meant to me, and then— and then I took off her hood and set her free.'

Her eyes searched his face. 'And she came back,' she murmured.

He nodded. 'She came back. What a hell of a moment that was! I mean, there's always that chance the first time you fly a hawk...'

'How did you—what did you call it?—man her?'

He smiled. 'I spent every free minute with her,' he said softly, the memory of that time bright in his eyes. 'I fed her by hand. And once she was used to me, I carried her everywhere on my fist. It took weeks, but eventually she trusted me.'

A slow smile tilted at the corners of Rachel's mouth. 'I never thought of it that way before,' she said. 'The hawk being afraid of you, I mean. I always think of hawks as aloof and powerful.'

David's arm tightened around her. 'Something can be aloof and powerful and still have needs, Rachel.'

She drew in her breath and looked up at him. The sun was on his face, softly blurring his rugged features. When she spoke, her words were a whisper on the still air.

'I . . . I know what hawks need,' she said. 'They need freedom.'

His arms encircled her. 'Isis came back to me,' he murmured, drawing her towards him. 'Can you imagine how it felt to see her dropping out of the sky, to know she'd chosen to be my captive instead of freedom?'

The blood felt thick in Rachel's veins. 'Yes,' she whispered. 'I can. It must have been wonderful.'

'Rachel . . .' There was only the single word, but it burned its way into her heart. 'Rachel,' he said again, his arms tightening around her, 'look at me.'

The whispered words were a command she could not deny. Slowly she raised her eyes to his and the breath caught in her throat. His golden eyes smouldered in his dark face, glowing with a desire so urgent that it made her tremble.

'David, no . . .'

Her plea was lost against his lips as his mouth covered hers. She gasped and tried to twist away from him, but his hands moved to her face, cupping it in a rough embrace and tilting her head back as he bent to her again. The touch of his mouth was even sweeter than she remembered, and she swayed within his arms as his kiss branded her with his need. But it was her need too, and she moaned softly as passion leaped within her, surging hotly through her body with every heartbeat. David's arms closed around her again, moulding her body to his. Her mouth slackened beneath the onslaught of his, opening willingly to his heated plunder, and his kiss changed, deepened, became something more intimate, more demanding than any she had ever dreamed possible. This was where she'd always been destined to be, she thought suddenly, in David Griffin's arms, warm and wanted and needed...

Suddenly he picked her up and cradled her to him in arms that crushed her against the muscles of his chest and while she kissed him, while her mouth opened to the sweetness of his tongue, he strode across the whispering grass to the shadow of a lone pine tree that stood like a dark sentinel in the centre of the meadow.

'Rachel,' he muttered thickly.

She closed her eyes as he set her slowly on her feet. Sensation overwhelmed her as she slid slowly down the length of his body, the straining hardness of him telling her that he wanted her as she wanted him. Cassie, she thought suddenly, but her mind was closed to her step-sister's name. Cassie had lied—she had lied before. There was nothing new in that. David was nothing like the man she'd described. He was...he was...

She gasped as he drew her jacket from her and slipped her hands under her blouse. His palms and fingertips were hot and rough against her flesh, arousing new waves of sensation. Her life had been so empty, so barren until this moment. How could she tell him that? How could she tell him what happiness he had brought her? How...

'Kak, kak, kak...!'

The hawk's cry was wild and exciting high above them. Rachel drew back in David's arms, her eyes focusing softly on his face.

'Isis?' she whispered.

He nodded, his face flushed, his eyes as hooded and dark as the hawk's had ever seemed.

'Yes,' he said thickly, 'she must have seen something...'

Leaning back in his embrace, she shaded her eyes against the sun as she stared into the sky. The hawk was overhead, her wings beating mightily. A dark speck flew beneath her.

'There she is,' Rachel began, then she drew in her breath. 'No,' she murmured, 'no...oh God, don't...'

The hawk fell on the dark object flying below her. The powerful wings beat once, twice, then Isis gripped the smaller bird, binding it to her in her sharp talons and bringing it to the ground. Rachel buried her face against David's chest.

'She killed it!' she whispered.

David drew her closer. 'Rachel, sweet,' he murmured, 'it happens sometimes. She's a hawk, she only does what she must to survive.'

Rachel shook her head. 'I know, David. But that poor bird—it never had a chance.'

His hand cupped her head. She could hear the steady beat of his heart beneath her ear.

'Nothing has a chance against a hawk, Rachel. That's just the way it is.'

The words and the truth in them beat against her heart like hammer blows. Dear God, she thought, what was happening to her? She drew a shuddering breath and stepped free of his arms.

'I...I'm going back to the house,' she murmured.

David smiled as he touched his finger to her mouth, swollen from his kisses. 'All right, Rachel. Let me call Isis in and... Rachel! Rachel!' His voice rose, but she ignored it, catching up her horse's reins and swinging into the saddle. 'Rachel, what the hell are you doing?'

She kicked the horse into a trot. 'What I should have done days ago,' she said, the answer more for herself than for him. 'I'm leaving.'

CHAPTER EIGHT

THE STABLEMAN'S face was a puzzled blur as Rachel slid from the saddle. 'Is everything all right, miss?' he asked, peering past her.

'Everything's fine,' she said, tossing him the reins. 'Mr Griffin will be along in a few minutes.'

The house was a still, cold citadel in the bright sunlight. It was best to do this before Emma got back, she thought, hurrying to her room, before she saw Jamie again.

Don't think about Jamie, she told herself while she pulled her suitcase from the closet. Just do what has to be done. All she'd managed these past weeks was to put off what had been inevitable ever since the night David had walked into her life.

Blindly she yanked a handful of dresses from the closet and tossed them into the suitcase. Jamie was David's son. She couldn't fight his right to the child, but she could fight what he was doing to her. Each time he touched her, she trembled with a desire so intense that it frightened her. She had never known anything like it before. The Snow Queen, Cassie had called her once, and it was true, she had never understood the flame of passion that other women felt or known the urgent need to caress and be caressed until now, and she feared her own confusion as much as she feared David Griffin.

Her face coloured as she remembered the way she had melted in David's arms only moments before. She could

still feel the touch of his hands on her body, smell the
maleness of him, taste his sweet mouth. Oh, God, she
thought, how close she'd come to giving herself to him.
It would have been a betrayal of Cassie's memory...
And yet he wasn't the sort of man Cassie had said he
was. He wasn't. He...

The brutal image of the goshawk swooping earthward,
its innocent prey clutched to its breast, intruded. 'Hawks
do what they must to survive,' David had said as if that
could explain the agony of the victim and the pleasure
of the hawk.

'Stop it!' she hissed to the silent room. There were
questions within questions, but only one answer, and
that was to get out of this house and do it now. It was
what she'd have to do eventually. Better to do it on her
own than to wait until David told her to leave. Jamie
was at home here, now. He loved David and he loved
Emma too. *Not more than he loves me,* Rachel thought.
But to think that way was useless. Jamie's memory of
her would fade, with time. It was she who would never
forget.

Tears pricked her lashes and she wiped her hand rougly
across her eyes.

'Come on, Rachel,' she said to herself, yanking open
the dresser drawers, 'get packed and get back to New
York, where you belong.'

She scooped her neatly folded clothes from the
drawers, tossing them carelessly into the suitcase. Not
that they were really hers; David had paid for all these
things. For a second she thought of leaving it all behind,
but then common sense prevailed. She had nothing else,
not even money. There had been a cheque from David
waiting for her each week, but the thought of accepting
money to care for Jamie had repelled her, and she'd sent
the cheques to a children's charity. It had seemed the
right thing at the time; now, it struck her as a prideful

gesture that had done nothing but guarantee poverty. Well, she thought, the first order of business would have to be a job. Maybe there was an opening at the company where she'd worked before Cassie had . . . before Jamie. Her typing might be a bit rusty, but . . .

Rachel spun around as the bedroom door crashed open, slamming loudly against the wall. David, his face cold with rage, stood in the doorway. Her heart thudded crazily and the clothing she'd been packing spilled from her hands.

'Did you ever hear of knocking?' she demanded. 'It's polite . . .'

'The hell with being polite! What do you think you're doing?'

She swallowed and turned away. Carefully she bent and picked up the things she had dropped. Don't let him intimidate you . . .

'What does it look as if I'm doing?' she said coldly. 'I'm leaving here.'

He kicked the door and it banged shut behind him, the sound rolling like a clap of thunder through the silent house.

'Leaving here?' he repeated, twisting the phrase until it sounded like an obscenity.

'Yes,' she said, not looking at him. 'I thought it was time.'

'Did you?'

She knew it was not a question, but she ignored it as a statement. 'Yes. I had to leave, sooner or later,' she said, concentrating all her energies on the suitcase, folding and refolding garments as if they were important to her. 'That was our agreement.'

'Our agreement was that you'd stay as long as I needed you.'

'I was supposed to stay as long as Jamie needed me,' she said carefully. 'And I did. But he . . . he doesn't need me any more. He's comfortable with you and Emma and...'

'A few weeks ago you were begging me to let you stay. You didn't want to think about leaving the boy, you said.'

His voice was cold and mocking. Rachel looked up at him. He was leaning back against the closed door, arms folded across his chest, staring at her. His face was a blank mask that told her nothing. Her eyes met his and then skittered away.

'There's no sense in prolonging it,' she said finally. 'Sooner or later...'

'You already said that.'

'It's the truth. I...'

'You decided this moment was the best time to leave?'

She drew her eyes from his and looked back at the suitcase. 'If that's how you want to see it, yes,' she said.

David's lips drew back from his teeth in a smile. 'Is there another way to see it? You decided to take the easy way...'

Rachel's head snapped up. 'The easy way? Do you really think that leaving Jamie is easy?'

David shrugged his shoulders. 'Running away is always easy.'

'You know damned well I'm not running! I just... I don't see any point in prolonging this. I have to go back to the real world eventually.'

He nodded as if she'd just announced a great truth. 'Ah, yes,' he said, every word icily sarcastic, 'you have to return to the real world. How foolish of me to have thought you could ever forget the Golden Rooster. Would you like me to help you get your old job back, Rachel?'

'I'm not going back to the Rooster.'

It was as if she hadn't spoken. 'Let's see—you'll need your costume. Well, that's a bit of a problem, isn't it?'

'David...'

'I mean, it's locked up in your old apartment building, and you'll have to pay your back rent before the landlord will give you your things. But we can solve that problem.' He reached into his pocket, a cold smile twisting the corners of his mouth. 'That should take care of things, Rachel,' he said, throwing some money on the bed. 'That ought to make up for the inconvenience of being so far from the bright lights.'

She looked down at the crumpled banknotes. 'What are you talking about?' she whispered, two spots of crimson riding high on her cheeks.

David shrugged. 'It can't be easy to be stuck out here in the middle of nowhere when you're used to crowds and people.'

Rachel stared at him incredulously. 'You know that's not why I'm leaving,' she said slowly.

'Yeah, well, you know what they say about sisters under the skin. You and Cassie would have similar tastes, wouldn't you?'

'I'm not like Cassie...'

His eyes were ice. 'Aren't you? All you can think of is yourself. The hell with Jamie, the hell with me...

'Damn you, David Griffin! I'm leaving precisely because of how I feel about you and J...' Triumph flashed across his face and Rachel spun away. 'Get out,' she whispered.

'So it's true,' he said softly. 'You're not just running, you're running scared.'

'You can call it whatever you like. I don't care...'

'I told you about running scared, Rachel. I said it was the surest way to draw attention to yourself.'

His voice was soft, almost a caress. She turned to face him, drawing in her breath when she saw the look on his face. She took an unconscious step back.

'I...I looked at the train schedule,' she said, her eyes refusing to meet his. 'If I hurry, I can make one at two o'clock.' She reached blindly towards the dresser and gathered up a handful of clothes. 'I'll pay you back for all this.'

'Why are you running from me, Rachel?'

'I'm not. I told you, it's time for me to go. I...'

'What are you afraid of?'

'Look,' she said quickly, 'this isn't getting us anywhere. I'm not afraid. I simply...'

He took a step towards her. 'Put that down,' he said softly.

She looked at the clothing in her hand and then at him. 'I told you, there's a train to New York at...'

'Put it down, Rachel.'

'I'm almost finished,' she said, taking another backward step. She ran her tongue across her lips as she felt the unyielding surface of the wall press against her shoulders. 'David, please...'

He was so close to her that she could see the pulse beating in the hollow of his throat. His mouth curved upwards in a lazy smile and he reached out and traced a finger across her lips.

'Please, what?' he murmured.

Rachel shut her eyes as he moved closer, his hand closing lightly around her neck. She could feel her pulse beating as rapidly as the wings of a frightened bird. Could he feel it? Did he know what was happening to her? When she spoke, her voice sounded faint to her own ears.

'Please go away,' she whispered.

His thumb stroked gently across her parted lips. What would he do if she turned her mouth towards his questing hand and pressed it to his palm? Rachel swayed as she imagined the heated flesh beneath her lips, the sweet, salty taste of him.

'Please,' she said faintly, but he only smiled.

'No more running,' he said, his voice thick and urgent. He took the garments she was holding from her nerveless fingers. Lingerie fluttered to the floor like bright ribbons falling from a woman's hair.

'David,' she said, 'I beg you...'

'Come to me, Rachel.'

'No,' she said, the word a sigh that hung in the silence. There was a wisdom in his eyes that made her tremble. Locking his fingers around her wrist, he drew her towards him. 'Yes,' he said, 'yes, that's right, love. Come to me.'

'Why are you doing this to me?' she whispered.

'I want to make love to you, Rachel. You know that— you've known it all along. It's what you want too.'

'No,' she said again, 'no, David...'

'Yes,' he said in a fierce whisper. 'Put your arms around my neck. Do it, or I'll do it for you.'

Her hands moved up his arms, across his shoulders, and laced behind his neck. She felt him tremble beneath her touch, and a surging power raced through her.

'David,' she whispered, and his arms closed tightly around her.

'David, what?' he asked in a husky whisper. 'Tell me what you want, Rachel.'

'I...I...' She swallowed and shook her head. His eyes were golden discs, the pupils black pools in which she would surely drown. 'I want...I want...'

She swayed in his arms and he pulled her against the hardness of his body, locking her to him in an embrace that made her gasp.

'Tell me you want me,' he whispered.

'I don't...'

But the whispered denial was meaningless. His hands moved up to cup her face, holding her captive for his kiss. The touch of lips scorched her flesh, and she moaned softly as his tongue traced the soft contours of her mouth.

'Tell me you want me the way I want you,' he whispered against her lips, 'tell me you want to feel me inside you.'

Rachel felt as if the world was exploding around her. Desire engulfed her, sweeping everything aside. Her arms tightened around his neck and she pressed her body to his.

'Yes,' she said, and the word was a triumphant song bursting from her throat. 'I want you. I want...'

His mouth covered hers, silencing her words. His kiss was wild and passionate, promising everything a woman could find in a man's arms. Her lips opened to the fevered touch of his tongue and when she was filled to overflowing with the wonderful sweetness of him, his mouth left hers and his lips touched the long column of her throat. Her neck arched as he trailed hot, moist kisses on her flesh, and she cried out when his mouth reached the soft hollow at the base of her neck.

'David,' she sobbed, 'David, yes, yes...'

She caught her breath as she felt his lips touch her breast through her silk blouse. Her hands, as if of themselves, curled into the thick, dark hair at the nape of his neck and pressed him closer to her. He whispered her name as his hands trailed down her back, then he cupped her buttocks and lifted her towards him. Rachel rocked forward, without any awareness of what she was doing, and moved her hips slowly against him. David's breathing became harsh and ragged.

'Rachel,' he said, 'love, I won't be stopped this time. I can't.'

It didn't matter whether the hoarsely uttered words were a promise or a threat. She knew only that they had left reason behind on the way to this moment and that it was too late to go back, for her as well as for him. There was a raging hunger within her heart and body. Where was the honeyed sweetness of desire that she'd read about? What she felt was a need so intense that it was almost pain. David's mouth and hands were teaching her secrets that burned her flesh; his whispers were promises that made her reckless with longing.

'I don't want you to stop,' she whispered. 'Make love to me, David—please!'

His soft laughter was the sound of conquest. Eagerly he swung her up into his arms and she gloried in the strength of his embrace, sighing when his fingers spread across her breast and cupped it, branding her as his. Beneath his palm, her heart was racing out of control. She clung tightly to his neck as he crossed the room with her and laid her gently on the bed. Sunlight filtered through the net curtains, filling the room with shifting shadows and reflections, making it seem almost like an underwater cavern. The bed felt as liquid as the sea— and why not? she thought crazily, why not, when she felt as if she were flying across the ocean, bound to her passions like a whalerman bound to a whale that was pulling him over the sea on a Nantucket sleigh-ride that might never end.

Her eyes opened and fastened on David as he stood beside the bed. She watched as he unbuttoned his shirt, letting the soft wool slip from his bronzed shoulders. His arms were muscled and golden in the soft sunlight; there was dark hair on his chest, tapering to a narrow V as it dipped beneath his denim jeans. Rachel's glance flickered lower; the fabric was pulled taut across his groin, and a quiver of apprehension danced in her throat.

'David,' she whispered, 'David, I . . .'

He knelt beside her and took her in his arms. 'Yes,' he said roughly, 'say my name, say it that way, Rachel, as if it was the only thing that mattered in the world.'

His hands were under her blouse, hot against her back, holding her to him so closely that her breasts flattened against his chest. She was drowning in sensation, drowning in passion, and all the while the yearning ache grew within her thighs and belly. His fingers fumbled at her blouse. She watched his face as the buttons opened to him, her breath quickening as she saw the darkening of his eyes, his excitement fuelling her own. The silk blouse fell open and he bent towards her, kissing her through the lace bra.

'Beautiful,' he said in a thick whisper. 'My beautiful Rachel...'

His mouth closed on her breast. She cried out at the sensation, but it wasn't enough. She wanted to feel his moist tongue against her bare flesh and she reached blindly for the front closure of the bra—but David's hands were there before her. The lacy fabric fell away from her, baring her breasts to his mouth and to his hands. He reached towards her and a flush rose on her cheeks. Rachel turned her head to one side, but David's hand cupped her chin and he brought her face towards him.

'Watch me, Rachel,' he said. 'Watch me pleasure you.'

He brushed his lips across hers and then bent slowly to her breast, kissing the rounded flesh gently, then touching his tongue lightly to the engorged tip. Heat flared within her.

'David...' She moaned his name softly as his mouth closed around her. Waves of sensation flooded through her and her body arched upwards towards him, seeking him blindly.

'Do you like that?' he whispered. 'That's only the beginning, love. There's more—so much more, so much...'

Rachel reached up to him and linked her hands behind his head, bringing his face down to hers, her mouth opening to receive his kiss. Every part of her was on fire. Nothing was enough—not his hands on her breasts, not his mouth on hers, not the feel of his hair-roughened chest against her nipples. Their dampened bodies were pressed tightly together, but she needed something more, something that would quell the flames blazing within her. She had never imagined anything could feel like this. People talked about sex, and she had read her share of books, seen her share of films, but... Not sex, she thought suddenly. Love. Oh God, oh yes, oh yes, she loved him, she loved David, she...

Her zipper hissed in the stillness. 'David,' she whispered, wanting to tell him, but he smiled and put his finger across her mouth.

'Don't be afraid, sweetheart,' he said softly.

'It's not that,' she said. 'I'm not afraid. I'm...oh, David, David!'

His hands were everywhere, touching her shadowed places, teaching her mysteries she had waited a lifetime to learn. Whatever she had wanted to tell him was forgotten. What did words matter, when their bodies spoke so eloquently?

'Rachel,' he said thickly, and then he was gone. Her eyes fluttered open.

'David?' she whispered. 'Don't leave me...'

'I won't, love,' he murmured. 'I'm right here.'

He was standing beside the bed. She watched as he stripped off his jeans and shorts. His body—that mysterious male body she had never seen—was beautiful. She had seen statues, but no sculptor, not even Michelangelo, could ever bring this warmth and passion to marble. David was hard angles and flat planes and taut muscle. Her arms ached to hold him to her and she reached up to him.

'Come to me, David,' she whispered.

His eyes were licks of golden flame as he bent over her. She sighed as he covered her with his body. There was a sudden, shivering pain and Rachel drew in her breath.

'Rachel,' he groaned, 'oh, love, I should have known! I should have asked...'

'Don't talk,' she whispered. 'Please, not now. Make love to me.'

Still he hesitated. Rachel sighed and began to move slowly beneath him, learning instinctively what women have always known, and then there was no time for talking, no time for thinking. Like a fragile shell on a distant beach, she was caught in a wave and swept far out to sea. The foaming water drew her under until finally, when life and death seemed to have joined together in one fierce moment, the wave scooped her up again and tossed her on the shore. She lay trembling in David's arms, her heart thudding in time with his, her hair lying wildly on the pillow in damp tangles.

He smiled at her and brushed his lips across hers. 'Are you all right?' he whispered.

Rachel nodded. 'I'm wonderful,' she sighed.

He laughed softly. 'You certainly are,' he said, and she blushed.

'You know what I mean, David. That was... it was wonderful!'

He smiled and stroked a damp curl back from her forehead. 'Why didn't you tell me you were a virgin?'

She laughed. 'It's not exactly dinnertime conversation, David! When was I supposed to have told you? Besides, what does it matter?'

'I wouldn't have...I'd have gone slower, for one thing.'

Rachel sighed. 'Any slower and I'd have died,' she said, then she blushed. 'Am I terrible for talking this way?'

David tweaked the tip of her nose. 'Stop fishing for compliments,' he said. 'I already told you you were wonderful.'

'Are you sure? I never... well, I never thought people joked afterwards. I thought it was all, you know, solemn and serious...'

'That's one illusion shattered,' he teased. 'What else?'

'Well, I...I never knew... I mean, I thought it took women a long time until they felt the way I feel...'

He smiled and ran his hand along her cheek. 'I'm glad it was good for you , Rachel.'

'I...I've never been so happy. In fact...' She drew a deep breath and rolled towards him, her body pressed against him. 'David...'

'I can make you feel that way again, Rachel,' he said, his voice thickening. 'I can make you feel even better.'

'No, you can't,' she began, wanting to tell him that loving him was what made her feel this way, but he silenced her with a kiss.

'I can,' he insisted.

Within seconds, she knew he had told her the truth.

CHAPTER NINE

'WHO'S my big boy?' laughed Rachel, swinging Jamie up into her arms.

The child's delighted shrieks filled the hall. 'Me!' he crowed, wrapping his arms around her neck. 'Me, Mama!'

'And who's going to let Emma give him his dinner and a nice bath, hmm?'

'No 'Nemma,' the boy said. 'You, Mama.'

Rachel gave him a quick hug and handed him into the housekeeper's waiting arms. 'Emma will let you play with your boats if you eat all your supper tonight, won't you, Emma?'

The woman smiled. 'I certainly will. How's that sound, lovey?' She shifted the child on her hip and nodded at Rachel. 'He'll be fine, Miss Cooper. You just go on and get yourself ready. It's almost five o'clock.'

Rachel looked at her watch in surprise. 'Already? Where did the day go? Mr Griffin said he'd be home by now.'

'You'd better get started, then, if you want to leave by half past,' Emma said briskly.

Rachel nodded. 'You're right. Go on now, Jamie. Emma will make you a jam omelette. How does that sound? And I'll be in to kiss you goodnight before I leave.'

'G'night,' Jamie sang happily, 'g'night, g'night...'

Rachel waved as Emma trundled him down the hall towards the kitchen. How had she let the hours fly away? she thought, hurrying to her room. And tonight was

132

special. David was taking her to a dinner in New York. Rachel had missed most of what he'd said. She was too excited at the prospect of going out with him for the evening. It would be the first time, unless you counted the night they'd gone to a movie in town.

'Is it going to be formal?' she'd asked, mentally running through the contents of her closet.

David had laughed. 'Terribly,' he'd said. 'Get Barton to take you shopping. Buy something gorgeous—I want every man in the room to envy me!'

She kicked off her shoes and looked at her new dress lying across the bed. It was long-sleeved and high-necked, a lush fall of burgundy velvet that looked very demure until she put it on. Then the soft fabric clung to her breasts and hips like a second skin. The saleswoman at Saks had said she looked wonderful in it, but nothing would convince her until David told her the same thing.

Rachel pulled off her clothes and padded barefoot into the bathroom. No wonder the day had gone so quickly! She had spent it shopping, going from one expensive store to another, searching first for a gown and then for bathing suits and sun dresses and outrageously high-heeled sandals. She stepped into the shower and turned her face up to the spray. She had never bought summer clothing in the middle of winter before. It had seemed like a decadent luxury, but David had insisted. They were flying off to Majorca tomorrow—he'd dropped that bit of news on the phone when he'd called that morning.

'Majorca?' She laughed in disbelief. 'I'm not even sure where Majorca is, David!'

'For shame!' he'd teased. 'It's just off the coast of Spain. We're going there tomorrow.'

'Just like that?'

'Just like that,' he'd laughed. 'Don't you like the idea of getting away from all this grey December weather?

'Well, yes, but it's so sudden—and what about Jamie?'

'Emma will take care of him.'

'And I haven't got any summer things, David, I . . .'

'Buy some.'

'But . . .'

'Rachel, I'm due back at a meeting. Stop arguing and do as I say. Believe me, after tonight we'll need a few days in some quiet hideaway.'

Rachel had shaken her head. 'David, I don't understand.'

His voice had dropped to a whisper. 'We'll have our own private beach, Rachel. Can you imagine how the heat of the sun will feel on your skin as we make love?'

Even over the long-distance wire, his murmured words had made her weak with desire. They had been inseparable the last weeks, although she wouldn't share his bedroom as he had asked her to.

'Emma will know,' she'd protested, and David had laughed. But he came to her each night. His arms sheltered her through the long hours of darkness, and his mouth kissed her to wakefulness each morning.

'Are you sure you aren't bored, living all the way out here?' he had asked her once, and she shook her head.

'I love it here, David. I have Jamie all day.'

His eyes had darkened. 'And at night?' he'd whispered.

'You know what I want at night,' she'd said shamelessly. 'You.'

His kisses had assured her that he felt the same way. She loved him—she knew that with an absolute certainty. And he loved her. He hadn't said so in as many words, but she knew. She was his safe haven, he said, his source of comfort at the end of a day in the trenches.

Rachel sat down at her dressing-table and looked at herself in the mirror. The man, the David her stepsister had described, had never existed, except in Cassie's imagination. David Griffin was good and decent. It amazed her that the man the newspapers characterised as 'the Hawk' could be happy with someone like her. But the tabloids didn't know that the Hawk liked to sit beside the fire with her hand in his, and spend hours in the falconry showing her his rare old volumes about hawking. She was even learning to feel comfortable in the mews, watching while he handled Isis and the other birds. There was a new falcon there now. A peregrine, David had told her, explaining that it was rare. A boy from town had brought it to him after finding it on the road, one wing dragging in the dust. Rachel had watched while the vet splinted it.

'A clean break, Mr Griffin,' he'd said. 'With luck, maybe this guy will fly again.'

The peregrine had hissed threateningly whenever David approached it the first few days, but he had persisted, speaking in soothing whispers, offering it bits of raw meat. He was 'manning' it, he told her, teaching it to accept him, and to her amazement, the beautiful creature was doing just that. Only yesterday the falcon had finally accepted food from David's hand and let him stroke its brown and white breast.

'I can't believe it,' Rachel had murmured, watching while the fierce creature fluffed its feathers in contentment. 'I never thought he'd let you do that.'

David's golden eyes had met hers. 'It takes patience,' he'd said softly, stroking the bird all the while. 'But it's worth it, Rachel. Taming a wild thing is a special pleasure.'

'I thought I was your special pleasure,' she'd said, her teasing immodesty making the colour rise to her cheeks.

David had grinned. 'Same thing,' he'd said. 'You're both my captives.'

Rachel had uttered a threat that they both knew she couldn't keep. He'd spoken the truth, she thought now, brushing mascara on her lashes. He had made her his own. She could be happy here for ever. A shiver of joy trembled within her. Tonight had to be important. He was going to introduce her to his friends. For such a private man, such an action spoke volumes.

She looked up as the door swung open and a smile lit her face. 'David,' she said softly. 'Welcome home.'

He smiled at her as he closed the door behind him. 'Hello, love.'

'I'm sorry I'm not ready yet, but I'll just be another few minutes. I was playing with Jamie and...'

'I like you just the way you are,' he murmured, bending to kiss her upturned face. 'You're just what a weary traveller should come home to.'

Rachel gasped as his hand slipped into the open neckline of her robe. 'David,' she whispered, 'what are you doing?'

He laughed softly. 'What do you think I'm doing?' His hand closed possessively around her breast. 'I'm saying hello to your mouth and your breasts and...'

She caught his hand as it moved downward. 'Stop that,' she warned, 'or I'll never be ready! You said we had to leave here by five-thirty, and it's past that now.'

He kissed the top of her head and straightened up. 'Spoilsport! All right, I'll behave. Give me five minutes to shower and change and I'll be back.' His glance fell on the burgundy gown, lying across her bed. 'Is that what you're wearing tonight?'

She nodded. 'Yes. Is it all right? The saleswoman said...'

He touched the velvet lightly and then held his hand out to her. 'It's perfect. I can hardly wait to see you in it.'

Rachel smiled as he drew her to her feet. 'I hope... I just want your friends to like me tonight, David. I'm so nervous.'

'Don't be,' he said quickly.

'I can't help it, David. I keep wondering what they'll think of me. I...'

He smiled and put his arms around her. 'They'll think what I think, Rachel—that you're beautiful and that I'm lucky as hell. I told you I wanted every man in the room to envy me when they see you.'

She laughed softly. 'That's very primitive, Mr Griffin!'

He brushed his lips against hers. 'And very satisfying. Their imaginations are going to work overtime. They...' There was a knock at the door and he frowned. 'Yes? What is it?'

'I'm sorry to bother you, sir,' called Emma, 'but Miss Walters is here. She's in the library.'

Rachel stiffened in David's arms. 'Vanessa's here?'

David sighed. 'Yes, she's going with us—I'm sorry, Rachel. Things are getting a bit pressured and she thought it best if she came along tonight.'

'Pressured? But I didn't think this dinner had anything to do with business. You said these people were friends of yours.'

'They are. But they're more than just friends.' He raked his hand through his hair and glanced at his watch. 'Look, we can talk tomorrow. This dinner—sometimes there are things you just have to do.'

Rachel laughed softly. 'I think you're suffering from jet-lag,' she teased. 'What you need is a cold shower.' She gave him a gentle shove. 'Go and get dressed. Now that I know Vanessa's going with us, I'll need an extra five minutes to get ready. She always looks so beautiful.'

'Not half as beautiful as you,' he whispered. 'No one is, Rachel.'

An hour and a half later Rachel and Vanessa stood in the foyer of the Helmsley Palace Hotel waiting for David to finish checking in their coats. Rachel repeated his words to herself like a talisman. But it wasn't working;

she had been intimidated the second she had come downstairs and found Vanessa waiting for her in a simple black silk gown that dipped as low in the back as it did in the front. And the women streaming past her into the ballroom were no comfort. They were, for the most part, older than she and obviously comfortable in these opulent surroundings. Jewels glittered in their ears and at their throats, and gowns that she had seen sketched in *Vogue* and *Elle* adorned their slenderly chic bodies. Her burgundy gown, so seductive at Saks, felt all wrong. And her hair—heavens, what had made her think she could simply wash it and brush it dry? It hung to her shoulders in dark waves. She probably looked like a gypsy, she thought unhappily, with her loose hair and her red dress. Unconsciously, her hand went to her head and she smoothed several errant curls back from her face. Vanessa glanced at her and smiled.

'Nervous, Rachel?' she asked softly.

Rachel nodded. 'Yes, a little. I ... I've never been to a dinner like this before. Will David be making a speech? I forgot to ask him.'

'Oh, yes,' the woman said. 'Thanks for reminding me. I've outlined a little something for him, just in case he's not prepared.'

Rachel was barely listening. Her eyes scanned the crowded foyer; she let out her breath when David finally appeared.

'There he is,' she whispered, smoothing down her skirt. 'Who's that man he's talking to?'

Vanessa gave her an amused smile. 'He's the senior Senator from New York, Rachel. Don't tell me you don't recognise him.'

Rachel flushed. 'Yes, yes, of course, now that you ... well, I mean, I've only seen him on television before.' She swallowed drily. 'Isn't that the Mayor? I didn't realise all these important people were going to be here. Why are you looking at me that way, Vanessa?'

Vanessa smiled. For the first time since Rachel had known her, the look in her eyes was friendly.

'Didn't David tell you anything about tonight, Rachel?'

Rachel shook her head. 'No, not really. Well, just that some people were giving this dinner for him.'

Vanessa stepped closer to her. 'I see,' she purred. 'I guess he thought he'd surprise you.' She smiled and laid a reassuring hand on her arm. 'Don't worry,' she said pleasantly. 'Everything will be fine.'

Amazing, Rachel thought. Life was filled with surprises. Even Vanessa Walters had a heart. Perhaps she'd simply misjudged the woman. David had said she was a top-flight assistant. And now, tonight, when Rachel most needed one, she was turning into a friend. Rachel managed a tense smile.

'I hope so,' she breathed. 'I don't want to embarrass him.'

'I tell you what, Rachel—why don't you and I make a stop at the ladies' room? Your hair's a bit dishevelled— I can fix it for you with some spray and... Ah, David, you're back. We saw you chatting with the Senator.'

David ran his hand through his hair and Rachel looked at him in surprise. *My God,* she thought, *he's nervous too.*

'What did you tell him, Vanessa?' His voice was low and irritated.

Vanessa shrugged her shoulders. 'Not a thing.'

His eyes flashed coldly. 'Don't push me, Vanessa.'

'I'm not pushing you, David. I'm advising you.'

'When I want your advice, I'll ask for it.' His voice reminded Rachel of talons cutting into a gloved fist.

David's face had darkened as he spoke. Rachel moved closer to him and cleared her throat.

'David?' she said anxiously. 'Is something wrong?'

'No,' he said quickly, slipping his arm about her waist, 'nothing you have to be concerned about, Rachel. I just want to clear some things up before we go in to dinner.'

'There's Secretary Pickering,' said Vanessa suddenly. 'You have to say hello to him, David. His office has been after us for weeks—he wants to talk to you about backing one of his projects.'

'Damn it, Vanessa—all right, all right, I guess I owe him the courtesy. Rachel, come with me.'

Rachel looked across the foyer at the famous face of the Cabinet Member and she shook her head. 'No,' she whispered, 'that's all right, David. You go on. I...I have to powder my nose.'

His eyes searched hers. 'You're not happy here, are you?'

'I'm fine,' she lied. 'Really, David, I'm just not good at this, that's all. I think you should have left me behind with Jamie.' She laughed nervously and leaned towards him. 'David, please—don't let me hold you back.'

'Listen to her, David,' said Vanessa. 'She makes sense.'

'I have to talk to you for a minute, Rachel.' His fingers bit into her arm as he drew her aside.

'What is it?' Rachel whispered, her eyes searching his face. 'David, I know something's the matter!'

'Rachel, look, I thought I could just let these people get a look at you tonight, but...' His fingers raked through his hair again and he sighed. 'You just have to get through tonight, and then everything will be OK. I...'

'David...David!' a rumbling male voice called across the room. 'Do you have a minute?'

Rachel took a deep breath. 'David, please—what are you talking about? Get through what? I don't understand.'

He touched his lips to her forehead. 'I'll explain tomorrow on the beach,' he said softly. 'When it's just you and me.'

'David...' Vanessa stepped between them, smiling brightly. 'I'm terribly sorry to interrupt, but the Secretary says he must see you before we go in to dinner.'

'Oh lord, Van...'

'You can't just ignore him, David. Don't worry about Rachel.' She smiled and patted his arm. 'I'll take good care of her.'

David looked from one woman to the other. 'Rachel?' he asked at last.

Nothing made sense. People were pooling around them, the women talking to each other in bird-like chirps, the men puffing cigar smoke into the air. She could hear some of them whispering David's name, feel their eyes boring into her. A coldness clutched at her heart. She was suddenly afraid, but of what? There was nothing to fear but fear itself. Wasn't that what Grandma used to say? Rachel forced herself to smile.

'Go on,' she said. 'I'll be fine.'

'I'll probably have to introduce you,' he said. 'The damned place is loaded with reporters. I guess that was the Senator's idea—it wasn't yours, was it, Vanessa?'

Vanessa shook her head. 'No, of course not.'

'Yeah—well, the Senator's people will want to milk this for all the publicity they can get. Look, Rachel, I'll try to keep the reporters away from you, but if they ask you questions, just do the best you can. You don't have to answer them if you don't want to. I...'

A sea of dinner-jacketed men closed around him and he was gone. Rachel's heart was pounding with an unknown terror. She turned towards Vanessa and laid her hand lightly on the other woman's arm.

'Please,' she whispered, 'what's going on?'

'It's all terribly confusing, isn't it?' Vanessa said soothingly. 'I can't believe David didn't tell you what was going to happen tonight.'

Rachel shook her head. 'Why on earth would reporters want to talk to me? Vanessa, do you know what this is all about?'

Vanessa slipped a comforting arm around Rachel's shoulders. 'Come on, dear, let's duck into the ladies'. I'll fix your hair and fill you in a bit.' She followed Rachel's frantic gaze towards the ballroom, filling now with people. 'It's all right,' she said softly. 'This will only take a minute. I promise.'

The two women hurried across the foyer and into the ladies' room. As the door swung shut behind them, Vanessa put her finger to her lips.

'One sec,' she said. Rachel watched in disbelief as she scurried through the room, peering into the empty cubicles. 'Right,' she said, 'we're alone.'

'Will you please tell me what's happening?'

Vanessa Walters sighed. 'This is so difficult, Rachel,' she said, staring at herself in the mirror. 'I hardly know how to tell you.'

Rachel came up behind her and stared at her reflection. 'Just tell me,' she said flatly.

Vanessa's eyes met hers. 'You're not going to like it,' she said softly.

A chill of apprehension raced up Rachel's spine. 'No news is good news', Grandma had always said. For the first time, she understood the full meaning of that simple statement.

'Tell me everything,' she said. 'I want to know.'

The Walters woman sighed. 'All right, Rachel. A faction in David's party wants him to run for Governor.'

Rachel stared at her. 'Governor! But David never said anything.'

Vanessa shrugged. 'I suppose he felt it didn't concern you. Of course, it does, in a way. That's what this is all about.'

'That's what *what* is all about, Vanessa?'

Vanessa frowned and bent towards the mirror. 'David's supporters think he has a good chance of winning.' She touched her finger to her tongue and then dabbed at her eyeliner. 'He has quite a name in business circles, of course, but he's not exactly a household word, although I must say I've managed to get him quite a bit of publicity over the past few months. He's gone to a recognition factor of seventy-two per cent as opposed to a year ago when he only pulled fifty-nine per cent. He...'

'For God's sake, Vanessa!'

The woman smiled and turned around. 'Yes, all right,' she said softly. 'I'll get to it. One of David's problems was lack of recognition. That one was easy. I got him some awards, dropped some titbits in the columns—but there was a second difficulty. A much rougher one.' She lifted her hand and frowned at her fingernails. 'Do you know David's nickname? What the papers call him?'

'No,' Rachel said impatiently. 'I mean yes, they call him the Hawk. What does that have to do with...'

'Everything,' snapped Vanessa. 'You don't vote for a man called "the Hawk", do you? People think hawks are cold-blooded killers—nobody wants that kind of person in government. All right, so we had an image problem, a tough one. You know how elections go in America—the candidate gets photographed kissing babies and eating pizza and everybody loves him. But it wouldn't work with David—he's too strong a personality for that. So we had to find a way to humanise him, to make people see him as a man with faults and strengths the same as anybody else...' She smiled coolly. 'Do you know what I'm saying, Rachel?'

A knot of fear had lodged in Rachel's breast. Grandma had been wrong, she thought crazily. There was more than fear itself to be afraid of—there was this dizzying sense of walking across a tightrope stretched across a yawning chasm, a tightrope that seemed never to end, only to stretch interminably into the darkness. She ran her tongue across her suddenly dry lips.

'No,' she said, 'I don't know what you're saying. Why don't you just spit it out?'

Vanessa smiled again. 'What I'm saying is that we had a problem with David's image—until your stepsister had the good grace to die.'

Rachel blinked. 'What?' she whispered. 'What did you say?'

'You heard me.' Suddenly the helpful tone of voice was gone and the old Vanessa was back—cool, precise, and calculating. There was a viciousness in her face Rachel had never seen before. 'When Cassie Cooper died, David told me about their...liaison. He said he wanted to know more about her child.'

'About...about Jamie? He told you...?'

A smile curled on Vanessa's red lips. 'Of course he told me. David and I have no secrets. You've been a diversion, Rachel, but diversions are only temporary. Sooner or later...'

'Tell me about Jamie,' said Rachel with single-minded determination. 'What happened after David told you about him?'

'I arranged for a private investigator to find out all about the boy. Within days we knew everything—that he was indeed David's son, and that his aunt, a barmaid, was raising him.'

Rachel took a deep breath. 'All right, Vanessa, I knew most of this. David told me he'd used a detective agency to find out about Jamie. But I still don't see what any of this has to do with tonight.'

'Believe me, tonight wasn't my idea.' The Walters woman's voice dripped venom. 'But David suddenly decided he wanted you along. What is it about men like David? Must they exhibit their trophies to the world?'

The colour drained from Rachel's face. 'How dare you?' she whispered. 'I'm not a... David and I... We...'

'You're just a bonus that came with Jamie. Don't you understand, Rachel? Jamie was what we needed. How better to humanise a man like David? We'd admit his error to the world—everyone's entitled to a mistake, after all. There he'd be, strong enough to admit his transgression publicly, loving enough to want his son...'

Rachel took a step backwards. 'No!' she said sharply. 'That's not true. David told me why he wanted Jamie. It was because he'd been an orphan himself...'

'He was, yes, that's true. I don't know why he told you. There wasn't any reason—well, perhaps there was,' Vanessa said slowly, her eyes fixing on Rachel's face. 'You can't expect to bed a woman by telling her you slept with her sister and walked out on her sister's bastard...'

Rachel's hand was a blur as it cracked against Vanessa's face. 'You're a liar!' she gritted.

Vanessa raised a hand to her cheek and the breath whistled between her teeth. 'That doesn't change anything,' she said softly. 'Let me tell you the rest. We took a poll and found that sixty-two per cent of our male voters would envy David for seducing a woman as lovely as Cassie Cooper. And you wouldn't believe the percentage of women who wished they'd been in her place. Of course, there was some risk, but...'

Rachel put her hands to her face. Could it be true? No, she thought, no... but it all made a terrible kind of sense. She could still remember her shock at David's sudden willingness to claim Jamie. And, although she'd shunted it aside, there was Cassie's version of her affair with David, Cassie's ugly, sordid tale of what he had done to her.

'No,' she said faintly, sinking back against the wall. 'I don't believe it. David isn't like that. He loves me. He loves Jamie...'

'He's developed a fondness for the boy. Amusing, isn't it? As for you, my dear Miss Innocent, yes, he's become enamoured of your naïveté. Of course, he'll tire of it soon enough. A man like David has appetites you can't possibly feed. And when he's weary of trotting home to you, he'll write you a nice fat cheque—for services rendered.'

Rachel's eyes blazed with fury. 'Lies, all lies,' she said angrily. 'You're jealous, Vanessa. You want him yourself.'

'Lies, are they? Well, try this one for size, Miss Cooper. David is going to tell the world about Jamie tonight.'

'No! He'd never do that.'

Vanessa shrugged impatiently. 'What did you think that double-talk was all about, Rachel? The Senator's been pressuring him, and I agree that the timing is right.'

'Is that why... why he said he'd have to introduce me?' Vanessa nodded and Rachel put her hand to her mouth.

'Now you're catching on. Don't look so panicked, Rachel. You won't have to say much to the reporters— just something about how grateful you are to David for rescuing you from a place like the Golden Rooster. And how hard it was to raise the boy alone. And then you and he can go back to your little love nest for a while and...'

Rachel closed her eyes. Yes, she thought, the man they called the Hawk would believe that. He had made her his captive, hadn't he? She would go on being his lover— *no*, she thought, *not his lover. His mistress*—and he'd have his party's nomination and the Hawk would have made another kill.

Cassie, she thought in despair, Cassie—forgive me. You were right. David Griffin was everything her step-sister had said he was. She took a deep breath.

'He used me,' she said slowly. 'He used me and he used my baby...'

'Oh, for goodness' sake, don't get melodramatic, Rachel! He did what he had to do, that's all.'

'I won't let him get away with this,' whispered Rachel. 'I'll...'

'You'll what? We've been in here too long. The speeches will be starting soon, and David's going to come looking for you. What are you going to do then, hmm? Make a scene? Give the papers headlines and photos that will haunt you and the child for years?' Vanessa paused and caught her lip between her teeth. 'Actually, I don't think David should have brought you here—I think it looks tawdry. If it were up to me, I'd slip you out the door.'

Something in Vanessa's voice made Rachel look up. Their eyes met, and Rachel understood she was being offered an escape from the nightmare that threatened to consume her. She took a deep breath.

'All right,' she said quietly. 'What do you want me to do?'

Vanessa smiled. 'You're not as naïve as you seem, are you? It's simple, really. I'll go into the dining-room and make some excuse to David. I'll tell him you ripped your dress and we're in here fixing it. And then I'll sneak you out of the hotel. I have...' She opened her purse and rummaged through it. 'I have almost five hundred dollars here,' she said. 'And I'll write you a cheque for five thousand more if you'll take a taxi straight to the airport and take the first plane out of New York. Don't go near the boy, don't contact David...'

'I can't. I . . .'

'There's a little shop in the hotel. I'll get you something less conspicuous to wear.'

'But I can't leave Jamie,' Rachel insisted. 'I love him.'

'He isn't yours to love,' the other woman said coldly. 'David will take good care of him. He's not a cruel man, Rachel. Surely you know that?'

Rachel closed her eyes against the sudden image of Isis plunging towards her prey. 'No,' she said. 'He simply does what he must to survive.'

Vanessa laughed. 'I wouldn't put it that way!'

Rachel slumped back against the cold tile wall. 'Put it any way you like,' she whispered. 'Just get me out of here.'

A triumphant smile blazed across the other woman's face. 'Well, well,' she said softly. 'Little Miss Innocent is growing up at last!'

CHAPTER TEN

How MANY films had Rachel seen in which someone jumped into a waiting taxi and said, 'I'll double your fare if you get me to the airport in twenty minutes'? But life wasn't like that, she thought as her taxi wound slowly through the city's Friday night traffic. There hadn't even been a taxi to jump into—it had taken the doorman a couple of minutes to whistle one to the door. Hurt and bewildered beyond measure, Rachel had scrambled into the cab and let Vanessa slam the door after her.

'La Guardia Airport,' Vanessa had said. 'And hurry!'

It seemed to take forever for the taxi to pull away from the kerb. Rachel expected to hear David's voice calling after her; she took her first easy breath only after half a dozen blocks separated her from East 50th Street. She laced her fingers together, trying to still the trembling of her hands. She could hear Vanessa's voice telling her all those terrible things about David, telling her how he'd lied and schemed and used her. Dear God, how he'd used her...

How could she have been such a fool? She had known what he was—Cassie had told her. But she'd chosen to believe David instead. A drunken tumble in the middle of the night, he'd said, with her stepsister as the instigator. No, there hadn't been any long, sensual seduction. No gifts, no long-stemmed roses. Just two willing people. Just quick sex.

A dozen pictures tumbled through her mind, pictures of herself and David in bed. It had been sex, yes, but it had been so much more than that. It had been love and need and caring—for her, she realised suddenly, but not for him. She moaned softly, remembering the abandon of their lovemaking. The humiliation of it was like a physical pain, sharp as a knife wound to the heart.

'I loved you, David,' she whispered into the darkness, 'I loved you...'

'Are you OK, lady?'

Rachel looked up and met the cab driver's gaze in the rear-view mirror.

'Yes,' she said carefully, 'I'm fine.'

'You sure? I thought maybe you said something...'

'It was nothing.'

'Look, if you're feeling sick...'

'I said I was fine, driver. Just get me to the airport, please.'

The cabby nodded, but she could see him watching her. She probably did look ill—she'd caught a glimpse of her pale face and mascara-smeared eyes in his mirror—and then there was the way Vanessa had all but shoved her into the taxi.

She laughed, the sound soft and bitter in the darkness. It didn't matter a damn what the cabby thought. Nothing mattered, not any more. She'd lost Jamie and she'd lost her self-respect, and she was to blame.

'Stupid,' she said softly, 'stupid, stupid...' She looked up and her eyes met the driver's again. She put her hand to her mouth and his glance slid nervously from hers.

Yes, she thought, stupid was the word to describe her. Naïve, Vanessa had said, but that was far too kind. Not that it mattered, really. Neither absolved her. What was that childish rhyme Grandma had taught her to chant? A real tongue-twister: 'She sells sea-shells on the sea-shore'—that was it. This had been a grown-up version of that rhyme. 'Cassie's seducer seduced Cassie's sister'... All it had taken was a different technique, and manipulation was David's business, wasn't it? Poor Cassie had tried to convince her of that.

Rachel shuddered and closed her eyes. The Hawk had known that what had worked with her stepsister wouldn't work with her. Cassie had been a fool for expensive restaurants and hothouse flowers, but she had simpler tastes. Long horseback rides in the Catskill foothills and longer evenings before the fire had been the key to her heart, that and seeing David's growing love for his son.

And he did love Jamie—even Vanessa admitted that. That must have come as a surprise to David and Vanessa, both. It had surprised her, at first. But even hawks had hearts. The past weeks had taught her that much—she'd seen David's birds respond to his touch. Why wouldn't he respond to the love of a child? Not that his feelings would stop him using the boy...

The story of Jamie's birth would be told with delicacy, of course. Vanessa would find a way to make the child's illegitimacy and Cassie's death sound romantic and tragic, and David would tell the story with just the proper degree of restraint and humility. There probably wouldn't be a dry eye in the room when he finished speaking. Too bad she wouldn't be there to say a few words and make him sound like a knight in shining armour who'd rescued her from a life of degradation at the Golden Rooster. Had he really expected her to do that for him? Rachel shuddered. Yes, why shouldn't he? she thought. She had done everything else, hadn't she? She'd turned her back on her stepsister's memory and let him do anything he wanted with her, anything...

'Dear God,' she whispered, 'help me!'

David Griffin had taken everything from her. Her sense of honour, her self-respect, her loyalty to Cassie— he'd stripped it all away. And he'd stolen her baby from her, for the most base reasons. All that nonsense about his own orphaned childhood—personal gain had been what had motivated him, not love. Rachel closed her eyes and shook her head. God, he was despicable! Her breath quickened. Anger was a safer emotion than pain, and she welcomed it and clutched it to her. Why had she let Vanessa persuade her to run away? She should have confronted David on his own turf. What satisfaction it would have given her to face him in the ballroom and tell him she knew the truth.

'I know what you are, David,' she'd have said. 'Cassie never lied to me. *You* were the liar, you heartless, selfish son of a bitch!'

Yes, she thought, yes. Quickly she leaned forward and rapped on the partition dividing passenger and driver.

'I've changed my mind,' she said. 'Take me back to the Helmsley Palace.'

The driver stared at her in the mirror, then nodded. Horns blared angrily as the cab came to a sudden stop, turned, and reversed direction. Rachel sat back, heart racing as she thought of the things she'd say to David. He wouldn't be alone, of course. He'd be surrounded by his rich and powerful friends. Fine. Let them all know what a bastard he was. And the reporters would be there too. Once they heard what she had to say, they'd be like vultures circling above carrion, waiting to devour anything the hawk had left.

The story would make all the newspapers. Jamie and Cassie would be named in a dozen lurid headlines, all of them a hundred times worse than any David's carefully worded announcement would cause. There'd be nothing romantic and tragic about the stories the papers would print; the circumstances of Jamie's birth would be made sordid and ugly. Jamie, she thought, Jamie...

Rachel sat forward and tapped on the partition again. 'Forget about the Helmsley Palace, driver. Just take me to the airport.'

The brakes squealed and the cab bucked to a halt. 'Are you sure, lady?'

Rachel nodded. 'Positive.'

'Because we've been uptown and we've been downtown and . . .

'The airport,' she said firmly.

The cabby sighed. 'OK, lady, the airport it is.'

Yes, she thought, this was the best way. She'd take a plane, any plane, and fly into the night and never again see the child who was as much hers as if he had grown beneath her heart for nine months.

'Stop!' The cry was so sharp that the cab driver responded without hesitation. The brakes screeched again and the taxi ground to a halt.

'I'm not going to the airport,' Rachel said.

The driver's eyes met hers. 'Look, lady . . .'

'I want to go downtown,' she said firmly. 'To 4th Street.'

Horns blared behind them, but the cabby ignored them. He sighed and turned towards her. 'Listen,' he said, drawing the glass partition aside, 'maybe you ought to let me take you some place where they can help you, huh? Bellevue Hospital's not far.'

Rachel lifted her chin. 'I don't need a hospital, thank you. Just take me to 4th Street.'

The man shrugged his shoulders. 'It's your money, lady. Where on 4th Street?'

'Near Christopher,' she said. 'I'll tell you where to stop when we get there.'

Her old apartment building looked more forlorn than ever. Rachel paid the cabby and then trudged up the stairs. If her former landlord was surprised to find her on his doorstep late on a Friday night, he didn't show it. At first, he was sullen and uncooperative.

'Come back Monday morning,' he told her. 'I'll open the storeroom then and you can get your stuff—after you pay me the rent you owe me. And there are storage charges, too, ya know. And...'

His mouth fell open when Rachel stuffed a hundred-dollar bill into his hand.

'Open the storeroom now,' she said. 'All I want is my clothing. You can sell the rest—it'll more than make up what I owe you.'

Finally, suitcase in hand, she climbed the stairs to Mrs Gould's apartment and knocked at the door. When the old woman opened it, she gasped in amazement.

'Rachel? Rachel—my goodness, where have you been?'

'I...I've been away, Mrs Gould. May I come in, please?'

'Of course, dear. What a nice surprise! I was worried to death about you. I came back from my son's house months ago and no one knew where you'd gone or... For heaven's sake, here I am, babbling like an old fool, and you look positively exhausted! How would you like a nice cup of tea?'

Rachel smiled wearily. 'That would be lovely.'

Mrs Gould bustled back and forth for the next few minutes, setting out sugar and milk and cookies on the low table before the couch. Finally she poured two steaming mugfuls of dark tea and handed one to Rachel.

'Now,' she said, 'tell me where you've been all this time, dear. They said you'd vanished into thin air.'

Rachel nodded. 'Yes,' she said, 'I...I went away rather suddenly. Someone...someone my stepsister had known came for Jamie and me.'

The old woman smiled. 'A friend of Cassie's? That's nice. How's my Jamie? And where is he?' She leaned forward anxiously. 'Is something wrong, Rachel?'

Rachel shook her head. 'No, no, everything is fine. Jamie is—er—he's staying with Cassie's friend for a while.'

'While you get settled, you mean.'

'Exactly. Mrs Gould, I know it's an imposition, but— might I stay here for the night? I'll be out of your way early in the morning, I promise.'

'Of course, dear. But you seem...are you ill, Rachel?'

'I'm just tired. It's been a long day.'

'Well then, let me get you a blanket and some pillows, dear. The couch has seen better days, but you're welcome to it.'

The old woman fussed over her until finally Rachel forced a yawn and pretended exhaustion. But once she was alone on the narrow couch, she lay staring into the dark. She'd come this far, but she had no idea of what to do next. She'd stay in New York, yes. That way she'd be near her baby. Maybe she could even get a glimpse of him, once in a while.

The thought was so pathetic that it brought tears to her eyes. But that hope was all she had left. Her entire world had collapsed around her. First she'd lost Cassie, and now she'd lost Jamie. And David...oh God, David! He'd come into her life and changed everything. Until she'd met him, she had thought Jamie's love was all she needed to banish the loneliness that had been hers most of her life. And then David had shown her another kind of love, a love that made her realise how incomplete her life had been...

What he'd shown her was that she was the worst kind of fool. Damn him to hell, she thought, punching her fist into the pillow, damn him, damn him...

By dawn, Rachel had neither tears nor anger left. She was numb; she lay in the chill of the early morning, trying to find a reason to go on living.

Take things one day at a time, Rachel.

Her grandmother had always said that. But what was the point? Her days wouldn't change. Each would be as empty as the last.

God provides for him that trusts, Rachel.

Rachel sighed. All right, Grandma, she thought, I'll give it a try. For a little while, anyway. And then we'll see.

At breakfast, Mrs Gould urged her to stay on.

'I'd enjoy the company, Rachel. Just you remember that if you can't find an apartment.'

Rachel patted the old woman's hand. 'You're very kind. Thank you.'

'What about your old job, dear? Will they take you back?'

'I'm not going back to the Golden Rooster,' Rachel told her without hesitation. 'I'll find something else.'

But there was nothing else, not for someone whose secretarial skills were rusty, and a clerical job wouldn't even cover the rent for the tiny apartment she finally found in a run-down part of the city. It was cheap, but not cheap enough, especially since she'd shredded Vanessa's cheque and flushed it down the toilet the night before. She didn't regret it, but it made her situation more desperate. Tears of frustration filled her eyes as she stood reading the 'help wanted' sign in the window of a bar that was a duplicate of the Golden Rooster. She had come full circle. The difference was that there was no Jamie to go home to any more.

She forced herself to get up each morning and go through the routines of the day. At night, she worked until her feet ached from teetering on her high heels. She filled in for anyone who wanted time off, working extra hours without complaint. But that was the way she wanted it; it meant that she fell into bed each night in an exhausted stupor, too tired to think or dream. She owned no television set and bought no newspapers, but every now and then David's picture leapt off a newsstand at her, once with a smiling Jamie in his arms. 'NY'S NEXT GOV?' the headline said, and Rachel turned away as a bitter taste flooded her mouth. David's ploy had worked, then. The Hawk had what he wanted.

There was a heavy snowstorm late in January, one bad enough to discourage even the bar's regular customers. At midnight, the owner closed up and told everybody to go home. Rachel took off her skimpy costume and pulled on her usual old cords and sweater. It was freezing out; she huddled under her coat as she hurried along the dark, icy streets. She hated these blocks between the bar and her apartment. Sometimes there were drunks lounging in the doorways. Not tonight, though. At least the weather had driven them off the streets.

The silence of the heavy snow had made the street a twisted wonderland. She was breathless as always by the time she reached the fifth floor of her apartment building. Her hands were numb with the cold—it took forever to fumble the key from her pocket and into the lock. And then, just as she swung the door open into the yawning darkness of her apartment, the hair rose on the back of her neck. Someone was lurking in the blackness at the end of the hall.

'Who's there?' she whispered. No one answered, but she heard the rustle of fabric. 'I...I'm not alone,' she lied, desperation roughening her voice. 'My date's going to be here in a second. He's just parking the car...'

'Then you'd better tell him to stay the hell away, Rachel,' said David, stepping into the light. 'I don't think you want anyone to hear us.'

'David?' His name was a whisper floating in the air between them. She felt her heart lurch against her ribs. 'David?' she said again.

He smiled in that cold way she remembered all too well. 'You always were a bright girl, Rachel. Yes, it's me.' He glanced down the staircase and then back at her. 'Where's your friend?'

She tore her eyes from his face and followed the direction in which he was looking. 'My friend? Oh, that... There's... there's no one. I just said that because I thought... I thought...' Rachel took a deep breath. 'How did you find me?'

David smiled again. 'Ah, Rachel, Rachel, you disappoint me. I told you money can buy anything. The same detective as last time—that's how I found you.' He nodded at the open doorway. 'Aren't you going to ask me in?'

'No,' she said. 'What for? What do you want, David? What are you doing here?'

He stepped past her and the darkness inside her apartment swallowed him up. 'One question at a time, please. And I have no intention of answering any of them in the hall.'

The light clicked on in the living-room. She blinked in the sudden brightness and then she moved slowly through the door. David stepped forward and slammed it shut behind her.

'This place makes your other apartment look like a palace,' he remarked, barely glancing at the peeling walls and stained chairs. 'I guess five thousand bucks doesn't buy much these days.' She watched, transfixed, as he walked from one end of the shabby room to the other, pausing before a framed photograph of Cassie. 'You really did love her a great deal, didn't you?'

'Look, David...'

'I just hope she was worth it.'

'Worth what? I don't know what you're talking about. I don't know what you're doing here... What's the matter? Do you need me for a testimonial? Isn't Jamie enough?'

His lips drew back from his teeth. 'Well,' he drawled, 'at last! I wondered if you'd ever get around to mentioning Jamie. You really had me fooled, you know. I mean, you did quite a job of convincing me that you loved the boy. But I was right at the beginning, wasn't I, Rachel? You didn't really care for him. He was just a burden Cassie had left you...'

But Rachel had stopped listening. The coppery taste of fear flooded her mouth. 'It's Jamie,' she whispered, moving towards him. 'It is, isn't it? Something's happened to him.'

David nodded. 'Yes,' he said grimly, 'something's happened to him. He had chickenpox.'

Her face whitened. 'Oh God!' she gasped. 'My baby—is he all right? Does he have a fever? Tell me, David! I...'

The golden eyes blazed with cold fury. 'Do you really give a damn? You didn't give a damn when you ran out and left him.'

She shook her head. 'I didn't run out. You know that...'

'You ran and never looked back. The hell with my son, the hell with me. You...'

'David, I beg you—what's wrong with Jamie? Please, tell me!'

'He's got Reyes' Syndrome,' he said, his voice flat and harsh. 'The doctor says his chances are fifty-fifty.' He took a step towards her. 'Will you come with me, Rachel? He...he cried out for you in his sleep last night.'

'Will I...' Her words ended in a sob. 'Please,' she begged, 'let's hurry!'

CHAPTER ELEVEN

THE CITY streets lay icy and dangerous beneath the snow. David drove with mindless abandon until they had twice spun out of their lane and into the path of oncoming traffic. Then he slowed the Jaguar to a pace that was merely terrifying. Rachel sat numbly beside him, staring into the stormy night. A dozen questions about Jamie raced through her head, but she was afraid to ask them, more afraid to hear the answers. Finally, as the lights of the city fell behind them, she turned towards David and ran her tongue across her lips.

'Is Jamie...' Her voice faded, and she cleared her throat. 'Does he...does he know you?'

David's fingers tensed on the steering wheel. 'I don't know,' he said flatly. 'The doctor says he's not comatose—not yet. But he doesn't respond to anything. He just...he just lies there...'

Rachel closed her eyes against the terrifying image. 'Is Emma with him?'

'Yes, of course. She's barely left his side.'

'Thank God for that!' she murmured. 'He must be so frightened—a hospital's a terrifying place when you're so little.'

'Damned right,' David said grimly. 'That's why I kept him at home.'

'At home? But...'

'The hospital wouldn't agree to let me stay with him. So I brought the equipment and the nurses and the doctor to the house until...until there's some change or...' His voice broke and he cleared his throat. 'You'd better buckle your seat belt,' he said gruffly. 'This isn't a hell of a good night for a drive.'

Rachel nodded silently. The snow was a maelstrom of whirling flakes, and she stared at it blindly, thinking of the first time she'd made this journey. So much was the same—it had been late at night then too. And she could remember sitting as far from David as possible, the same as she was now. And yet so much had changed. Then, she had looked at his shadowed profile and seen only a stranger. Now she felt herself remembering the taste of his mouth, the feel of his skin against hers . . .

Stop it! she thought, pressing her forehead against the cold of the window. She was remembering the wrong things. Think about how he used you, she told herself. Think about how he stole Jamie from you. Think about all the things Vanessa told you that terrible night . . .

Anger embraced her, and she welcomed it like an old friend.

'Can't you go any faster?' she demanded.

David's head swivelled towards hers. 'Do you want to drive the damned car? I'm trying to get us there in one piece. A hell of a lot of good you'll do Jamie if you end up lying on a slab in a mortuary!'

She knew he was right. The roadway was a frozen ribbon curling treacherously into the dark, and the snow was piling up at an alarming rate. What would happen when they reached the narrow, winding roads ahead?

'What if the roads aren't passable?' she asked.

He answered without hesitation. 'We'll make it.'

Yes, she thought, watching his shadowed face, they would. Once David Griffin set his mind to something, he succeeded. She, of all people, knew that. Tonight she was grateful for that determination. If only she could be as certain they'd reach her baby in time . . .

'Tell me about Jamie's illness,' she said, forcing aside the sudden fear that assaulted her. 'Chickenpox, you said . . .'

David nodded. 'Yes, that's right. A mild case—some spots, a little fever—and then, just when he should have been getting better, he began to throw up. His fever came back, and it climbed higher and higher. It was Reyes' Syndrome . . .' He slammed his fist against the steering wheel and his voice became harsh. 'Who in hell ever heard of Reyes' Syndrome?'

'Isn't there anything they can do?' whispered Rachel.

'They've done it. They've run out of medical miracles.' He glanced at her in the half-light from the dashboard. 'That's why I came for you,' he said coldly. 'I'm willing to try anything now. And when Jamie called for you last night . . .'

For the moment her anger displaced reality. 'Why did you wait so long?' she demanded, twisting towards him. 'Why didn't you contact me when he first became ill?'

His laughter was mirthless. '"The best defence is a good offence," eh? Isn't that another one of good old Grandma's snappy sayings?' He glared at her in the shadowy darkness, and the hatred in his eyes drove her back into the corner of the seat. 'How the hell was I supposed to contact you? With a crystal ball? I wasn't even sure you'd agree to come with me tonight.'

Her mouth fell open in disbelief. 'You what? Are you crazy, David? My baby needs me . . .'

'Oh, that's touching. Such tender feelings, Rachel! Isn't it a little late? Where was all that devotion when you left him?'

'You're a fine one to talk about devotion, David! You can lie to the rest of the world, but I was there when you first came for Jamie, remember? It certainly wasn't devotion that made you do that. And devotion had nothing to do with why you took him away from me.'

He flung a hand towards her. 'Listen,' he growled, 'spare me the speeches, right? They don't mean a damn, and frankly, even the sound of your voice makes me sick. All I'm interested in is pulling Jamie through this.'

Rachel stared at him and then she nodded. 'Believe me,' she said in a broken whisper, 'that's exactly how I feel.'

'Good,' he snapped. 'At least we agree on something.'

Yes, she thought, as silence settled around them, at least they agreed on something. Tears slid down her cheeks and she brushed them away with rough haste. Grandma used to say that the deeper you loved, the deeper you hated, but Rachel had never understood the truth of those words until this moment. The pain of David's betrayal was still as fresh as if it had happened only yesterday, and she despised herself for being so weak.

Endless minutes went by until the final stretch of twisted road lay ahead of them. She held her breath while the Jaguar laboured up the steep incline, sliding and skidding with stomach-wrenching abruptness, until at last they were through the iron gates and in the driveway. The car had barely come to a stop before she was out and hurrying to the front door. It opened as she reached it, and Barton's worried face appeared before her.

'Hello, Miss Cooper. I'm glad you . . .'

She touched his arm as she brushed past him, David's footsteps pounding behind her as she raced up the stairs. But when she reached Jamie's room, her courage almost deserted her. A coppery taste flooded her mouth and she hesitated, her fingers curled around the doorknob. Suddenly David's hand was on her shoulder.

'Are you all right?'

His touch was impersonal, his concern only that she be strong for Jamie's sake, but still she could feel his strength flowing into her. She squared her shoulders and nodded.

'Yes,' she said, 'yes, I'm fine.' Composing herself, Rachel opened the door and stepped into the room.

The teddy bears were gone. What had been a nursery was a hospital, crowded with oxygen tanks and metal trolleys bearing basins and syringes. Bambi and Thumper peered down from the wallpaper like alien creatures from a distant planet.

Emma was standing beside the crib. She turned towards the door and her face lit with relief.

'Thank you, Lord,' she murmured, as a white-uniformed figure rose from a chair beside Jamie's crib.

'Has there been any change?' David demanded.

The nurse shook her head. 'No, sir—none.'

The woman said more, a litany of counts and medications, but Rachel heard her as if in a dream. Reality was centred on the child lying before her. Jamie was on his back, his arms at his sides, a blanket drawn up to his chin. A transparent tube led from an oxygen container into his tiny nostrils.

'Jamie,' Rachel said in a choked whisper, 'Jamie...' She moved towards him slowly, hands outstretched, fighting to keep the tears from spilling down her cheeks. 'Is he—is he asleep?'

The nurse glanced at David and then at Rachel. 'Well, yes, in a sense. He...'

'He has bad dreams when he sleeps on his back,' she murmured, knowing how foolish that was even as she said it. The unnatural position, the shallow rise and fall of the little chest, told her more emphatically than words ever could that her baby was desperately ill.

She grasped the crib rail and bent over it, whispering soft words of reassurance she knew Jamie couldn't hear, then she put her hand against his cheek. His skin was hot and dry, as if an unholy fire were consuming him.

'He's burning up,' she said, raising frightened eyes to the nurse.

'He's getting antibiotics, and there are orders to start him on intravenous fluids if...'

David brushed past the woman. 'It's been two days now,' he said in a harsh voice. 'Two goddamned days, and he hasn't responded to anything. The doctor says...' He broke off and looked around the room. 'Where is the doctor, dammit? I thought I told him...'

Emma laid her hand lightly on his arm. 'In the next room, Mr Griffin. He had to get some rest. I promised to wake him if there was any change.'

Rachel's eyes sought David's. 'Isn't there anything you can do?' she pleaded.

And the Hawk, the man for whom nothing was impossible, shook his head in defeat.

'No,' he whispered, 'nothing. Not a goddamned thing.'

Rachel nodded, then she reached into the crib. 'He won't die,' she said quietly. 'I won't let him.'

'You can't take him out of there, miss...'

'Let her do as she likes,' growled David. 'My son is dying, dammit!'

'Yes, sir, but...'

'Go have some coffee. Or take a nap. Do something— do anything. Just get the hell out of here!'

'Mr Griffin...'

Emma took the woman's arm. 'Come along,' she said softly. 'We can both use a cup of tea.'

The door whispered shut behind them. David watched in silence while Rachel lifted Jamie into her arms and held him against her breast. The child was limp and unresponsive.

'Jamie?' Rachel whispered. She brushed her lips against the boy's forehead. 'Jamie, sweetheart, it's Mama.'

'Damn it, Rachel!' David's whisper was hard as stone. 'How can you do that?'

Her eyes flashed as they met his. 'How can I do what? I love Jamie with all my heart.'

'Sure. That's why you abandoned him.'

'Maybe you can explain why you took so long to tell me my baby was this ill,' she said in a furious whisper. 'Two days, you said... Why didn't you send for me? And never mind the crystal ball nonsense, David. We both know you can do anything you set your mind to. You found me once before—wasn't finding me this time as important?'

His eyes narrowed. 'Put my son down,' he said with soft menace. 'Put him back in the crib and get the hell out of here.'

'All right,' she said quickly, 'I...I'm sorry. I didn't mean...' She looked at the child in her arms and her eyes filled with tears. 'That was unfair of me,' she said softly. 'It wasn't your fault. I know I should have contacted you, left an address...'

David's shoulders slumped wearily. 'It doesn't matter,' he said. 'The boy wanted you and you're here. That's all that counts.'

'Yes,' she said softly, looking at the still child in her arms again and kissing his cheek, 'that's all that counts.' She bent carefully over the crib and placed Jamie in it. 'Thank you, David. I'm grateful.'

'Damn you to hell, Rachel Cooper!' Her name sounded like a curse on his lips. 'Don't waste your breath thanking me. I did this for Jamie, not for you. If it were up to me, you could have rotted in hell before you ever saw my son again. I would never have come for you if I weren't desperate. I thought maybe if you were here— if there was a chance Jamie knew it...if he...'

His voice broke and he turned away from her. Rachel took a hesitant step towards him.

'David, I understand. I know how you feel. I love him, too. I...

'David, I understand. I know how you feel. I love him, too. I...'

'Do you? Yeah, I suppose you do. Hell, I guess even you have some human feelings, Rachel. But don't try telling me you know how I feel.'

'But I do,' she protested. 'I love Jamie...'

His voice was thick with disgust. 'You love that sister you've enshrined,' he said. 'And you love yourself. Everybody else is a poor second.'

'That's not true!'

But he wasn't listening. He brushed past her and stalked to the crib, his face softening as he looked down at the child.

'I love you, son,' he said, his lips grazing the boy's forehead. When he straightened, his eyes fastened on Rachel. 'Outside,' he said coldly, jerking his head towards the door.

Rachel glanced into the crib. 'All right,' she murmured, 'just for a minute.'

She followed David into the hallway and he turned towards her, his face impassive.

'There won't be any more of what just went on in there,' he said without preliminary. 'It was stupid of me. For all I know, the boy can hear what's going on around him.'

Rachel nodded. 'All right. We can talk out here, or downstairs if we...'

'We don't have anything to talk about,' he said sharply. 'Our only common interest is the boy's welfare.' His eyes, fierce and golden, sought hers. 'That's right, isn't it?'

'I...I... Yes,' she whispered, 'that's right.'

He nodded, then took a deep breath. 'All right, then. Just so we understand each other—I'd like you to stay as long as . . . until there's some change.'

'I have no intention of leaving,' Rachel said quietly.

'Fine. I'll tell Emma to prepare your old room.'

'No,' she said quickly, 'no, I'd rather sleep in the nursery.'

'Very well.' He started towards the stairs, then he paused. 'I'm going to send the nurse back up and ask Emma to make me some coffee. Shall I have her bring you some?'

Rachel glanced into the nursery. Jamie hadn't moved; he lay as still as before in his crib.

'She doesn't have to bother. I'll have it in the kitchen. Just as long as the nurse knows where she can reach me . . .'

'The kitchen? Is that where you'll be?' She nodded, and David's lips drew back from his teeth. 'Fine. Then I'll be in the falconry.' The wolfish smile vanished. 'Perhaps I should have made myself clearer, Rachel. You're here for Jamie's sake. I want no part of you.'

God, how he despises me, she thought, and suddenly, inexplicably, tears filled her eyes.

'David . . .' she began.

'I want nothing to do with you. Do you understand?' He took a step towards her. 'Do you?'

Rachel nodded. 'Yes.' The whispered word was like the rustle of dry leaves.

'I hope so. If I'm in one room, you sure as hell better be in another. Only the nursery is excepted.'

Tears trickled down her face, the salty taste of them filling her mouth.

'You'd like it to sound as if I'm the villain, wouldn't you?' she whispered. 'But I'm not. I . . .'

'What the hell's wrong with you, Rachel? I'm not interested. Don't you understand?'

'You're incredible,' she said brokenly. 'You—you use people, you twist things around, you...'

David moved towards her quickly, his shoulders hunching, his head angling downward. Suddenly Rachel remembered Isis, dropping like a stone from the sky, her talons extended towards her hapless victim. Her heart thumped against her ribs and she took a step back.

'I'm not afraid of you,' she said quickly.

The doorjamb pressed into her shoulders and she felt her heart flutter in her chest. David reached for her and she flinched as his hand encircled her throat, the thumb resting lightly in the hollow of her neck. She could feel the rapid skitter of her pulse beneath his fingers; he could feel it, too, she knew, because a cold satisfied smile touched his mouth.

'Aren't you?' he asked softly.

She shook her head. 'No,' she lied, as his grip tightened. 'No, I'm not. I...'

His smile widened until she felt as if she were looking into the cold face of death itself.

'Then you're a fool,' he whispered.

Rachel closed her eyes. When she opened them again, he was gone.

CHAPTER TWELVE

'THE MORE things change, the more they remain the same.' It was a French saying, not Grandma's, but Rachel thought nothing more aptly described the next hours. She had been an unwelcome guest in this house months before, and now she was one again. Still, there was a difference. When David had brought her here the first time she had lived in terror of his suddenly focusing those golden eyes on her and ordering her to leave. But she had no such fear now, and not just because he'd told her she could stay until there was some change in Jamie's condition. Rachel's thoughts had already ranged far beyond that. As the hours passed and the dark night gave way to the greyness of morning, she sat in the rocker beside the crib and plotted what she would do once her baby was well.

Each scenario had drawbacks. The simplest was to wait until Jamie recovered—and he would recover, she told herself fiercely—and then, in the midst of some dark night, walk out of the house with him and flee to the safety of a big, faceless city like Chicago or Dallas. The problem with that plan was that she couldn't imagine David allowing her to get away with it. Well, she thought, there was always the Press. She'd threaten David with exposure, tell him she'd give the newspapers the real story about him and Cassie and the hell with what it would do to Cassie's reputation...

Amazing, she thought, leaning her forehead against the bars of the crib. One plan involved kidnapping, the other extortion. But that didn't matter. She'd do what she had to do to get her baby back. She *would* get him back—and no one, not David Griffin or King Kong, would ever take him from her again. For now, she'd sit beside him, watching him as he breathed, touching him, kissing him . . .

Her head dipped forward and she blinked back from the edge of sleep. The doctor was beside her, bent over Jamie, a length of rubber tubing in his hand.

'What are you doing?' whispered Rachel, rubbing her hand across her burning eyes.

'Making the boy more comfortable,' he told her, jabbing a needle into Jamie's arm. 'I'm going to give him some fluids intravenously.' He glanced at her drawn face and shook his head. 'Get some rest, Miss Cooper. You can't keep this up for ever.'

'Yes, I can,' she said with grim determination, feeling the sting of the needle as if it were entering her own flesh instead of the baby's. 'I'm not leaving Jamie.'

It was the first time she'd given voice to the promise she'd made herself, but not the last. When Emma came to bring her a cup of tea later, she accepted it gratefully, but when the woman offered to relieve her of her vigil for an hour, Rachel shook her head.

'I'm staying with Jamie,' she said carefully. 'I'm never leaving him again.'

She heard a sharp intake of breath and she raised her head and peered into the shadowed darkness beyond the lamp. David was staring at her from across the room, something indefinably raw in his expression. For a moment, Rachel dared not breathe. She knew it had been a stupid thing to say with him there; she'd have to watch herself. But finally his eyes slid from her to the child in the crib, and her breathing returned to normal.

Careful, Rachel, she told herself. *Don't give anything away . . .*

But exhaustion had loosened her tongue and dimmed her mind. She made the same defiant promise to the nurse and then again to Barton when he tiptoed into the room hours later, and finally, when she was so weary that she could no longer tell if it was night or day outside the snow-encrusted window, she lowered the crib side, lifted Jamie into her arms, and whispered the promise to him too.

'Please come back to me,' she begged, touching her lips to his cheek. 'Please, Jamie! I swear I'll never leave you again.'

There was a stirring in the darkness and suddenly David stood before her. His eyes were shadowed pools, his face gaunt angles beneath a stubble of dark beard.

'Don't lie to him,' he said roughly.

'I love you, Jamie,' she whispered, ignoring the man opposite her. 'Do you hear me? Mama loves you.'

'Damn you, Rachel! I told you the boy might be able to hear us. Don't tell him lies.'

Her eyes met David's. *Careful,* she told herself, and then a combination of weariness and defiance flared within her and she said everything her tired brain could no longer censor.

'It wasn't a lie. It was a promise.' The words once spoken filled her with a great sense of peace. For the first time in months, Rachel smiled. 'Do you understand? No one will separate my baby and me again.'

David's face darkened and his fists curled at his sides. 'That's enough,' he growled, moving towards her. 'For God's sake, Rachel...'

'Mama?'

The soft word was barely audible, but it cut between David and Rachel, silencing them with its power. Rachel bent towards the child in her arms, afraid to believe he had spoken.

'Jamie?' she whispered.

The child's eyes fluttered open and fastened on her. A rapturous smile spread across his face and he reached a chubby hand towards her cheek.

'Mama,' he said happily.

A sob caught in Rachel's throat; she pressed a kiss against the childish palm and then touched her lips to his forehead, where dampness suddenly glistened.

'His fever's broken,' she said, her voice quavering. She raised her eyes to David's and laughter bubbled in her throat. 'He's going to be all right!'

David touched the boy's cheek. 'Thank God,' he whispered, then he bent and kissed Jamie's cheek. 'Welcome back, son,' he said in a husky whisper.

The child's smile broadened. 'Daddy,' he said, and his hand reached up to touch Rachel's face. 'Don' go 'way, Mama,' he sighed as his eyelids drooped closed. 'Please!'

Rachel clutched the exhausted little body to her breast. 'Never,' she said without hesitation. 'Never, never, never...'

She raised her head, ready to tell David that she would see him in hell before she gave Jamie up again, but he was staring at her with such a peculiar expression on his face that the words caught in her throat. His golden eyes, fiercer than Isis's, burned into hers. Was he challenging the promise she'd made? It didn't matter; not all his money or power would separate her from her baby again. Turning away, she hugged the child to her and sank into the rocker.

'I won't leave you,' she whispered. 'I swear it.'

Dawn broke in the snow-filled sky and still Rachel sat with the baby in her arms. The doctor had examined the child, smiled and pronounced the crisis ended.

'I'll put him into his crib,' the nurse had said, reaching for Jamie, but Rachel had snatched him from the doctor's arms.

'No,' she'd said firmly, settling the baby at her breast. 'I'll hold him.'

For the next few hours Emma and the nurse came and went. Only David stayed constantly. Rachel was dimly aware of his presence, knew it was he who drew a blanket over her, he who held a cup of tea to her lips and urged her to drink, but her concentration was for Jamie alone, as if she could make him draw strength into his body from hers. When finally the nurse persuaded her to hand the baby over so she could change him, Rachel stood, wincing as her aching muscles protested the long hours of inactivity.

'You need some rest, Rachel.'

David's voice was hoarse with fatigue. She looked at him and shook her head.

'I'm fine,' she told him.

'You're going to get sick if you keep this up!'

'Don't be silly,' she insisted, shaking her head. 'I . . .' But shaking her head had been a mistake. Incredibly, the room was spinning around her. 'David?' she whispered, then she tumbled into a black void.

Rachel awoke in a room filled with the thick silence that comes only in the middle of the night. She lay still for a moment, wondering at the feel of the unfamiliar bed beneath her. A soft white glow was coming from a window beside the bed. Moonlight, she thought hazily, moonlight reflecting on a fresh fall of snow... Her lashes drifted down and touched her cheeks—and then, suddenly, the past hours came rushing back. She sprang up in the bed, trying to untangle herself from the clutch of the bedclothes.

'Jamie!' she gasped, panic in her voice. 'Jamie...'

A shadowed form stirred in the gloom. 'He's fine, Rachel.' A match whispered in the darkness. A candle glowed into life and came wavering towards her. David smiled at her from within the pool of golden light. 'It's all right, Jamie's sound asleep. The nurse is with him.'

'What happened to the lights?'

'The storm took the lines down.' The flame flickered as he set the candlestick on the bedside table. 'Would you like something? Coffee or tea—a sandwich, perhaps? You've been asleep for hours.'

'No, nothing, thank you. I... What time is it?'

'Two in the morning. You passed out, and then...' He raked his fingers through his hair. 'I...I want to thank you for what you did.'

Rachel shook her head. 'I didn't do anything. His fever just broke, that's all.'

'Yeah, that's the doctor's story, too. But...well, I think it was more than that. And I...I just wanted you to know I'm grateful to you for coming.'

'Grateful?' Anger sharpened her voice. 'I love Jamie, David. Haven't you figured that out yet?'

'Look, I don't want to pick a quarrel with you, Rachel. All I know is that I almost lost my son and you gave him back to me.'

In the unsteady glow of the candle David looked worn and weary. The scar beside his mouth stood out in pale contrast to his unshaven face; the lines radiating from his eyes seemed more pronounced. Rachel's anger faded.

'You look exhausted,' she said softly. 'Haven't you slept at all?'

He shrugged his shoulders and sat down on the edge of the bed. 'A little. I dozed off in the chair for a couple of hours.'

'What you should do is go to your room and...'

'I am in my room,' he said with a quick smile. 'The doctor was using yours, so I brought you here.' He put his hands to his forehead and rubbed his temples lightly. 'I don't know what I'd do if anything happened to the boy!'

His voice was rough with emotion and weariness. Without thinking, Rachel reached towards him, her fingertips grazing his shirtsleeve. He raised his head and his eyes met hers. Her heartbeat quickened. *Are you crazy, Rachel?*

'Just give me a few minutes and you can have your room back,' she said. 'I...'

'Rachel,' David whispered. He shifted his position beside her and his thigh brushed against her hip. A shock raced between them, burning from his flesh to hers despite the layers of bedclothes separating them.

'Don't,' she said. 'Please, let me get up...' She drew in her breath. 'Who...did Emma undress me?'

David's eyes met hers. 'I undressed you.' His eyes darkened. 'It isn't as if I haven't done it before.'

Her heart tripped against her ribs. Yes, she thought, he'd undressed her before. She could still remember the last time. They'd been in the library, lying before the fireplace. The heat of the fire blazing in the hearth had matched the heat of their passion as David had slowly stripped away her clothing, prolonging the final seconds until she had thought she would die of wanting him. Her eyes met his and she knew he was remembering too.

'Rachel,' he said thickly, 'Rachel...'

He bent towards her and ran his hand lightly across her blanket-covered body from hip to breast. She felt herself quicken beneath his touch. Dear God, she thought, what kind of woman was she? How could she respond to him after all he'd done to her? But she was responding; there was that familiar tightness forming in the pit of her belly and that languid heaviness flooding through her veins and...

She pushed his hand aside and clasped the blankets to her. 'Let me up, David. I want to get dressed.' He said nothing. His hand had reached her throat; she shut her eyes as it closed lightly around her neck. 'Don't,' she begged. 'Please, don't!'

'Why not?' His voice was husky, the words softly blurred. He shifted position again until he was beside her, bent over her in the shadowed darkness. 'I know you want me, Rachel. Why pretend you don't?'

'No,' she breathed, 'it's not true.'

His hand slid to the back of her head and he drew her up from the pillow. 'Stop lying, damn you! Can't you be honest just once?'

His voice was rough, his hands insistent. Rachel twisted her head to one side, but his fingers threaded into her hair and forced her face towards his. She saw his eyes burning with golden fire as he bent to her, then his mouth covered hers in a hard kiss. She struggled furiously, but his hand held her fast while his lips parted hers, his teeth sharp against the tender flesh just inside her lower lip, his tongue relentless in its pursuit of hers. Pain lanced through her heart, a pain far greater than that which David was inflicting on her mouth and body. How could she have thought she loved this man? How could she have believed he loved her? How...

A low moan caught in her throat. Against all her wishes, her mouth was softening under his, her hands were reaching for him, sliding under his shirt to touch the familiar skin and muscle beneath. And even as Rachel cursed herself for having sunk to some sub-human depravity, her arms were sliding around David's neck, drawing him down to her, down into a darkness and a passion that would swallow them both.

'No!' Rachel's cry pierced the silent darkness. Her hands fell from his shoulders and knotted into fists. She pounded against his chest with all her strength while tears of rage and frustration slid down her cheeks. 'Get away from me,' she gasped. 'Damn you, damn you!'

'It's too late for that,' growled David. 'I told you that once before. You can't stop me, Rachel. And you can't stop yourself, either.'

He caught her wrists in one hand and pinned her arms above her head. The other hand grasped the blanket; she gasped as he ripped it from her. He said her name again and then his head dipped to her throat, his lips hot and moist against her skin. She cried out as his hand cupped her breast and his fingers rolled across the engorged nipple. David's lips sought hers, silencing her cry, taking the desperate plea into his own mouth, mingling her breath with his, turning her desperate cries from fear to desire.

'Rachel,' he whispered, drawing her to him, and she sobbed his name, caught in an all-consuming flame of passion she could no longer escape.

Later, she lay unmoving beneath him, stunned into lethargy. How could she have done this? Whatever Cassie had been, she—Rachel—was worse. To want a man like this... She ran her tongue across her dry lips.

'Get up,' she said. Her voice was unrecognisable to her, but then why wouldn't it be? The woman she had become was a stranger, a creature of lust and ugly passions. 'Get up,' she repeated.

He rolled away from her and lay on his back, his arm thrown across his eyes.

'I'm sorry, Rachel,' he said, his voice empty of all emotion. 'I shouldn't have done that.'

She reached to the foot of the bed and grasped the bedspread, wrapping it tightly around herself as she got to her feet. 'It doesn't matter.'

David swung his feet to the floor. In the flickering candlelight, his face was marked with rage.

'Of course it matters!' he snarled. 'What kind of woman are you that you can reduce me to this? I've never forced myself on a woman before.'

'No,' she said, 'that's not your style, is it? You prefer seduction.'

'God, are we back to that? I never seduced a woman who didn't want to be seduced in my life. I...'

'Look, spare me the details, all right?' Rachel grasped the ends of the spread between her breasts and reached for her clothes. 'If you'd call a cab for me, please...'

'Just like that?'

'Just like that,' she said, pulling on her cords. Her voice grew muffled as she drew on her sweater. 'That's if the phone is working. If not, would you please ask Barton to... What do you think you're doing?' she demanded, gasping with shock as David's hands closed around her arms.

'What a bitch you are,' he said in a voice so quiet it made her blood chill. His hands slid to her throat and closed around it. 'I could kill you, do you know that? No court in the world would convict me.'

'That's right,' she said, fighting to sound calm, 'no court would do anything you didn't want it to do. Not with all your money.'

'That's the second time you've mentioned money, Rachel. Are you leading up to something? Is the five thousand Vanessa gave you gone already?'

'I threw her cheque away,' she snapped. David laughed and colour flooded her cheeks. 'Ask her, if you don't believe me. Ask her if I ever cashed her cheque.'

His hands fell from her and he smiled. 'You never make a false move, do you? I can hardly ask her when I don't even know where she is.'

Rachel's eyebrows rose. 'What do you mean, you don't know where she is? She's never ten feet from your side...'

'She quit. The last I heard of her was a request for a letter of reference from some Congressman. So I can't very well ask her about the cheque you demanded, now can I?'

'*I* demanded?' Rachel laughed softly. 'What kind of story did she tell you, David? I was in no condition to demand anything that night. It was a miracle I was able to walk.'

'Look, just get your things together and get out of here, will you? I'll make up some story for Jamie. He'll cry—but he'll survive.'

Rachel drew her shoulders back. 'I meant what I said before. I'm not giving him up, not this time. I don't know how I'll fight you, but I will. I...'

'Listen, that speech may have impressed the hell out of Emma and the nurse, but it doesn't mean a damned thing to me,' snapped David. 'I know the truth, remember? Vanessa told me everything.'

'You still haven't told me why she left you, David. Did you tell her you wouldn't make her the Governor's lady? Is that what happened?'

The room was lightening as dawn spread over the Catskill foothills. In the paleness of the hour, David's face was a study in disbelief.

'Are you crazy? Vanessa and me...?' He shook his head and laughed unpleasantly. 'I'd as soon have made love to a cobra as make love to her! Oh, she was brilliant when it came to public relations, but she had a heart the size of a grain of sand!'

Rachel looked at him in surprise. 'But she said...well, it doesn't matter. I'm just surprised she'd leave you just when you were about to get what you both wanted. I guess it's a foregone conclusion that you'll get your party's nomination and then win the election.'

He shook his head again. 'Don't you read the papers, Rachel? I'm not seeking the nomination. I told the powers that be that I'd turn it down if they offered it.' He raked his fingers through his hair and his teeth showed in a quick smile. 'Which explains Vanessa,' he added. 'After I told her I'd rejected the nomination, she beat a quick retreat.'

Rachel sank slowly into the chair. 'But I saw a headline. It said you'd be the next Governor.'

David shrugged. 'Nobody believed I really wasn't interested. Hell, I can't blame them. But I'd made up my mind—long before that night at the Helmsley Palace, now that I think about it. But it all came together then and I decided to tell the Senator and Vanessa and...' His eyes met hers. 'Never mind,' he said gruffly. 'It's all water under the bridge, as your grandmother would have said. Just do me a favour, will you? I'll give you my attorney's name. Let him know where you are, so I can find you in case Jamie should ever...'

Without realising what she was doing, Rachel put her hand to her heart.

'The night at the Helmsley Palace,' she said slowly. 'Do you mean the night you took me there?'

A muscle jumped in his cheek. 'What other night would I mean?' he asked harshly.

She swallowed. 'You told them you wouldn't run that night?'

David nodded. 'Yeah, damned right I did. I thought the Senator would kill me, and Vanessa—well, Vanessa couldn't have really been surprised. She'd known what was coming. She was upset and angry and tried her damnedest to talk me out of it.' He walked to the window and stared out at the pale pink sky. 'It's almost sun-up,' he said softly. 'The snow's stopped.'

'David?' He turned towards her and she took a breath. 'David—did you make an announcement that night?'

He frowned. 'An announcement? About not running, you mean? No, I'd never made one about wanting the nomination, so...'

'No, not about that. About...about Jamie...'

He shook his head. 'What kind of announcement would I make about Jamie, Rachel? Hell, I'd told Vanessa a dozen times how proud I was of him, how I wanted to tell the world he was my son, but I couldn't think of a way to do it without letting everybody know he'd been illegitimate. Not that it mattered a damn to me—but I wasn't sure you could handle it. And then there was Cassie and how much she'd meant to you. Besides, I was afraid something like that might hurt the boy in later years...' A strangled sob escaped from Rachel, and David took a step forward. 'What is it?' he asked slowly. She shook her head and put her hands to her face. 'Come on, Rachel, what's wrong?'

'Vanessa told me—that night, Vanessa told me you were going to tell everybody all about Jamie, about your affair with Cassie and how you were his father...'

David's head shot up. 'What? Why the hell would I do that?'

'She said... Vanessa said it was because you and she had decided to soften your image. She said there'd been a problem with getting voters to stop thinking of you as the Hawk... She said that had been your plan all along, that you'd never really wanted Jamie until you realised it made political sense...'

His breath hissed through his teeth. 'And you believed her?' he asked, his voice ominously soft.

'I... I didn't know what to believe, David. You were so strange that night, nervous and... You said you'd have to introduce me, that the reporters might want to talk to me... When Vanessa said it was about Jamie—well, it made a terrible kind of sense.'

David's eyes met hers. 'It had nothing to do with Jamie,' he said. 'When I told the Senator I didn't want the nomination, he wanted to know what could be more important than public office, and I told him.' He gave a short bark of laughter. 'Funny, isn't it?'

Rachel shook her head. 'I don't understand,' she whispered.

David made an impatient gesture. 'Come on, stop playing innocent! I wanted a life with you, not the Governor's mansion. I wanted a home and children and...hell, what's the difference? All I knew was that I hadn't told you a thing about the nomination because I was unsure about it myself, and I didn't know how you'd feel about it. It never occurred to me that there'd be no keeping things quiet once you walked into that ballroom until I saw the Senator's reaction. So I tried to warn you, tried to explain...'

Rachel swayed under the shock of his words. 'You mean—you were trying to tell me that the reporters would ask about our relationship?'

He nodded. 'The reporters, the Senator—yeah, I figured they'd ask you our plans, and I didn't want you to think you had to answer any questions you didn't want to answer.'

Vanessa had lied. It had all been lies, vicious lies...

Suddenly David's hands shot out and grasped her shoulders. She gasped with pain as he pulled her from the chair. 'But, you had me so convinced! I thought— I thought you felt the same way. I never dreamed you'd... How in hell could you have done that to me, Rachel? Pretending to love me, to want me, when all the time, all the time you were just waiting for the right minute to humiliate me.'

His hands were hurting her, his fingers bruising her skin, cutting into her flesh, but the pain in her heart was far worse. He'd loved her, he'd loved her—and she had hurt him—oh God, she had wounded him and left him without a word, and all because she'd been willing to believe Vanessa, all because she'd still not admitted to herself that Cassie had never been any good, never, not even when they were children...

What was he saying now? Vanessa had told him lies within lies; she had told David that Rachel despised him, that she had only been waiting for the best moment to avenge her stepsister.

'Was it the sight of those reporters? Was that what made you decide to put your plan into action, Rachel? Was that why you picked that moment to leave me?'

Rachel shook her head. 'No,' she whispered.

'Don't lie to me,' he growled. 'Vanessa told me how you made veiled threats to tell the world I was the reason Cassie had turned to drugs and died. She told me about the cheque she wrote you, the clothes she bought you in the hotel...'

'David, please,' she begged, reaching out to him, 'David, my darling, my love...'

'Five thousand dollars and a goddamned dress,' he said brokenly, 'that was all it took to buy you off and send you away. God, Rachel, wasn't what we had worth more than that? Wasn't Jamie's love worth more than a stupid act of vengeance?' His fingers bit deep; she winced with pain as he shook her. 'I loved you more than I'd ever dreamed a man could love a woman. Nothing mattered but you and Jamie! I realised I didn't want to be Governor. I didn't want anything that would take me from you, Rachel. And all the time, all the time you were scheming and planning...'

Rachel shook her head. 'No,' she whispered, 'it's not true. I didn't do any of those things, David. I was so in love with you that I forgot there was another world out there.'

'What? What did you just say?'

Her eyes met his and searched for understanding. 'I loved you, David. I loved you with all my heart.'

'But...then how could you have believed Vanessa's lies? How could you have believed I'd hurt you?'

Her eyes filled with tears. 'I...I don't know. Maybe it was because it had been hard for me to believe that someone like you could love someone like me. Maybe it was because Cassie's ghost still haunted us. Whatever it was, I beg you to forgive me, David.' Tears spilled down her cheeks. 'I know it's too late for us—I know I've destroyed everything—but you must forgive me. I should never have believed Vanessa.'

'I'm as guilty as you are,' he said slowly. 'She made fools of us both.' His hands spread across her shoulders and drew her forward. 'The world is full of fools,' he said softly. 'And the greatest fools are those who refuse to forgive and forget.'

Rachel smiled through her tears. 'That sounds like something my grandmother would have said!'

David laughed softly. 'I told you I would have liked that old lady.' He smiled into her eyes. 'I forgive you, Rachel,' he whispered.

'And I forgive you, David.'

'See how easy that was?' He bent his head and kissed her tear-stained eyes. 'This past month has been such hell...'

Rachel shook her head and put her hand across his mouth. 'I don't even want to talk about it,' she murmured.

David smiled. 'All right, we won't. Let's talk about the future. Our future.' His hands cupped her face and he tilted it up to his. 'I love you,' he said softly.

'Yes,' she sighed, 'and I love you, David.'

'Will you marry me, Rachel?'

Her arms curled around his neck. 'Oh, yes,' she said, 'yes!'

His arms closed around her and he drew her against him. 'We'll turn this house into a home, darling, a home for you and me and Jamie...'

Rachel shook her head. 'No,' she whispered.

David drew back and stared at her. 'No?'

'No,' she repeated, then she laughed softly. 'Why are you limiting it to the three of us? I want at least two more boys and two girls.'

He laughed. 'Have you no shame? What am I going to do with you?'

Rachel sighed and brought his head down to hers. 'I'll show you,' she whispered, 'right after we say good morning to our son.'

EPILOGUE

THE HAWK soared high over the green meadow, its shadow skimming darkly across the summer grass.

'Look, Mama,' the little boy said, tugging at his mother's hand. 'See how high up he is!'

The dark-haired woman shaded her eyes with her hand and looked up into the cloudless sky.

'I see him, Jamie,' she said, squeezing his hand lightly in hers. 'Isn't he beautiful?'

The boy glanced up at the handsome man beside him. 'Are you sure he'll come back, Daddy?' Anxiety sharpened his four-year-old voice.

The man smiled and ruffled the child's hair. 'I'm sure, son. Just be patient.'

The man's arm closed around the woman's shoulders and she looked up at him and gave him a radiant smile. Suddenly the child standing between them danced with excitement.

'Look,' he said breathlessly, 'look, the hawk! He's coming back!'

The man smiled as the dark speck appeared in the sky again. 'Sure,' he said confidently. 'Didn't I tell you? He'd rather be captive than free.' His glance strayed to the woman. 'That's how it is, if you're lucky,' he said softly.

'Very lucky,' Rachel agreed.

David smiled and laid his hand possessively across the gentle swelling of her belly.

'I love you, Rachel,' he said, as their unborn child kicked against his palm.

'I love you, David,' she murmured, covering his hand with hers.

Jamie tugged at his father's leg. 'Everybody loves everybody,' he said with childish exasperation. 'Now, could we please get our hawk and have our picnic? I'm hungry!'

David and Rachel laughed, and David raised his gloved fist to the sky. High above him, the hawk cried out its pleasure and hurried earthward.

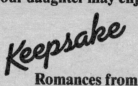

Harlequin Superromance

**Here are the longer, more involving stories you
have been waiting for . . . Superromance.**

Modern, believable novels of love, full of the complex
joys and heartaches of real people.

Intriguing conflicts based on today's constantly
changing life-styles.

Four new titles every month.
Available wherever paperbacks are sold.

Harlequin Intrigue

Two exciting new stories each month.

Each title mixes a contemporary, sophisticated romance with the surprising twists and turns of a puzzler...romance with "something more."

Because romance can be quite an adventure.

Intrg-1

Romance, Suspense and Adventure